the
promise
of a
normal
life

Also by Rebecca Kaiser Gibson

*Girl as Birch*
*Opinel*

# the
# promise
# of a
# normal
# life

## A NOVEL

## Rebecca Kaiser Gibson

ARCADE PUBLISHING • NEW YORK

First Edition

This is a work of fiction. Names, places, characters, and incidents are
either the products of the author's imagination or are used fictitiously.

Arcade Publishing books may be purchased in bulk at special discounts
for sales promotion, corporate gifts, fund-raising, or educational purposes.
Special editions can also be created to specifications. For details, contact
the Special Sales Department, Arcade Publishing, 307 West 36th Street,
11th Floor, New York, NY 10018 or arcade@skyhorsepublishing.com.

Arcade Publishing® is a registered trademark of Skyhorse Publishing, Inc.®,
a Delaware corporation.

Visit our website at www.arcadepub.com.

10 9 8 7 6 5 4 3 2 1

Library of Congress Cataloging-in-Publication Data is available on file.
Library of Congress Control Number: 2022943205

Cover design by Erin Seaward-Hiatt
Cover illustration: © ByM/Getty Images

ISBN: 978-1-956763-33-1
Ebook ISBN: 978-1-956763-61-4

Printed in the United States of America

To those who understand more than they know

All, says Buckminster Fuller, is angle and incidence.
—Guy Davenport, *The Geography of the Imagination*

# CONTENTS

# PART ONE

**1967**

# wait

There's a picture of me, at eighteen, on the boat to Israel. I'm wearing a white-ribbed wool dress and looking really thin and tan. I'm gesturing to my companions at the table. They all seem to be listening to me! Alice, the French girl, is next to me, and Devora, with her wide Israeli face and black hair, who was going to be a lawyer, is across from us.

I had just finished my junior year in England. On the last day of the term, the lowering gray sky had suddenly cleared to a light fresh rain, and then sun. The University of Sussex blossomed with students and faculty carrying transistor radios and listening intently to the news in Israel. It turned out to be a war that lasted only six days. I was walking down a gravel path to my dorm room, listening to the damp crunch of each step of my blue shoes and enjoying the bright rim of clouds around the first sunset in days, when I saw Professor Schiff striding dramatically toward me. Professor Schiff was American, a friend of my uncle, married to a British woman.

They had once invited me for tea, and I had walked tim-idly around their house full of miniature American carousels with hand-painted ponies and full-sized gumball machines equipped with early American candies. Schiff looked and acted like Leonard Bernstein. His long gray coat swooped from side to side with each step, without apology. He was larger than life and handsome. So when the dazzling Schiff approached and asked me, by name, and in a slightly chal-lenging and matter-of-fact voice, if I'd be going to Israel now that the war was won and the holidays started, I answered, "Yes," just because he'd acted as if I was there, a real person, a grown Jew. Just because I could not think, suddenly, of any reason not to; it seemed such an adventure, so stirring, so like what someone should do. After all, I had just started to read Doris Lessing's *The Golden Notebook*, the first book I'd ever read from my own point of view, a young woman's. I expected my parents to forbid me to go to a war zone, though I'd been to Israel years before at a summer camp with my sister, and I was surprised when they didn't. Their voices on the scratchy international line seemed very far away.

I flew to Paris, then took the train down to Marseille, equipped with a map and Doris Lessing. From the day my father had driven me to college in the Midwest two years before, I felt as if I'd sailed out from under a brooding cloud that had always draped me.

Then I was spending mornings at the American Express office in Marseille trying to get passage to Israel. It was just a matter of waiting, and I quickly adapted to the day's order. Eventually, a ship would have room for me if I kept returning and waiting in line. The harbor sparkled in the morning. Sometimes, I even got letters sent through the American Express office. One from Joyce told me that our parents were fighting, that they'd played a good game of tennis the day before.

Another letter arrived from a young man I'd met through a cousin the year before, when I was working at an ad agency in New York for the summer. Ben was also going to Israel after the Six-Day War. He was going to stay with relatives. I wrote back that I was trying to get there too. I wrote back more because I was proud to have a destination than because I cared about Ben. Especially in contrast to the sexual explicitness of the Lessing book, Ben seemed paltry. I had spent one night with Ben at his parents' house when they were out of town. We'd been to a Brahms concert in the Botanical Gardens, and it was late. He'd tucked me into his sister's bed and sat beside me as I drifted into a cottonwood blossom sleep.

There was nothing else I needed to do. My year of essay writing at Sussex was done. Nothing I needed to read, nothing I needed to explain. And I had a plan. I only had to wait until a ship became available. The sun of southern France fell on the mosaic floor of the American Express office. After my morning wait, I would walk—invisibly, I felt—in the crowds of international travelers. In the afternoons, I slept on the rocky beach, the sun beating into my brain until I was woozy. Afterward, to cool myself, I had ice cream by a river where French families seemed to have endless picnics like the ones in the Renoir films. The tables were small round ones, and I sat alone. At night, I ate *steak frites* by the harbor, then retreated early to a little room at a local university. In the morning, the sun reflected off a gold dome outside my single window. The sun, after months in the cold gray of England, was mesmerizing. And finally, after two weeks of waiting, a ship had room.

———

There were strawberries for breakfast on the ship and bright oranges that said "Jaffa" in small print, in English, JAFFA, JAFFA, JAFFA. Unlike the Sunkists I was used to, whose navel peel fell into the palm, these Jaffas were tenacious. When I bit, a bright orange-red taste sprang to my tongue. At my table, Devora and Alice were returning home to Israel. At eighteen, the same age as me, Devora was already a woman. Her hair was thick, sexual somehow. Devora welcomed us, her table-mates, to the trip to Israel, to the table full of food, to our whole lives from then on. Devora did not even bother to hold the round and friendly mound of her belly in tight, as I had been taught. Alice, however, wrapped her thin arms around her waist. She wore skirts that flipped, Frenchly, I thought, at her stride. Alice painted her toenails red. Alice put an icy blue hand on my glowing one. "Are you going to the dance?" she asked. I ate my lox and bagel in measured bites, claiming possession of the table. Alice waited for me to answer.

Bob and Celia sat at their own table, next to us. They were married; on Celia's finger was a big ring. Celia was Israeli but looked like Audrey Hepburn. Celia's skin was cupped to her, tightly pale; it rounded her cheekbones and sank closely into dimples. Her hair was tidy and short, a neat straight cap on her diminutive head. Celia was a nurse. Bob had graduated from Columbia. Thus were their credentials established for me. Bob's neck jolted out of his clean white shirt, like American boy necks I knew from westerns and college. Cosmopolitan Bob and Celia read bestsellers in English. They smiled, wearing duplicate cat-eye sunglasses.

Alice repeated, "There is a dance in first class, and we could sneak up to it, after it starts." A stowaway bee buzzed over my breakfast, feasted on the open orange segment.

*This is where I belong*, I thought.

That night the moon draped the silky water in ribbons. Alice and I waited under warm stars. Alice was sheathed in a slinky garment with a black cashmere shawl held tight. "Allons-y," said Alice when it was dark enough to escape tourist class. We streaked up the rubberized steps to first class. I, who was experiencing the whole trip as a dream, was imagining the late-night movies my father always fell asleep watching. I expected to see the couples leaning, in black and white, in simultaneous arching bends. I expected the dark cuffs of the men's dinner jackets, the definition of their jaws against the Breck-halo hairdos of their partners. The dancers would skate over polished floors, the violins would lift waves from the sea.

At the top of the stairs, I noticed that the door was marked, in three languages, DO NOT ENTER. I heard violins and entered. Inside, lights above the small dance floor, cool as blue moons, reflected softly off the scuffed floor. I saw

Alice, her skinny form already pressed like tape against the buttoned front of a man, her bony white arms dangling over his shoulders. Next to her, a gorgeous couple laughed. The woman, a blond decorated in rhinestones and wearing a gold lamé gown, touched the man with her long fingernails. I recognized her as the ship's social director. The woman gestured in my direction, the man looked at me. He was breathtaking, his hair a dark velvet, his skin smooth and dark. Minutes later, I sensed his dark suit by my side. The man introduced himself as Jacov, smiled with onyx eyes, and offered a glass of wine. We stood together, silver cup almost touching silver cup full of cool dark wine.

"I work for the ship," Jacov whispered, his voice fluttering over my head, his breath soft. "I take care of people on the ship." Dancing with him, I imagined hundreds of butterflies nestled, like my hand, in Jacov's. "I am the ship beautician," he said. "I do hair."

I tried to keep my breath calm, letting the words step into position. "I should come to you for mine then." Mine had been scorched dry while strolling the Mediterranean shore in Marseilles.

"It is lovely," Jacov said, professionally. He raised his cuffed wrist toward my hair. It hovered there, dipped as if to rest on my shoulders, then dropped to his side. He did not touch me.

"When could I come then?"

Jacov smiled. A waiter bowed in his direction, slightly. Jacov's smile sparkled everywhere. I loved it flickering on me. He was all booked up, he told me.

"How about lunchtime?" he asked. *Lunch together*, I thought, pleased, imagining the white napkins of first class, the crusty bread, wondering what I would tell my tablemates. "I think I am free over lunch, if you would not mind," he finished.

Why would I mind? The sangria was flattening the sharp edges of my mind.

"Mind," he added, as if reading mine, "if you came to the salon over the lunch hour."

The next day, the beauty salon surprised me since, of course, it was not built as one, but was a regular cabin with the beds removed and dryer chairs installed. No one else was in the salon.

"Lunchtime," Jacov reminded me, shutting the door behind me, gesturing to a green vinyl chair. Jacov released the chair top, which leaned back with barge-like majesty, presenting me head first to the deep porcelain sink. My shoulders eased of their own accord against the green, my eyes fell shut. My head rocked easily on the fulcrum of Jacov's hands. Jacov held my head in his hands and began to shampoo, rubbing with tumbling thumbs so that behind my eyes, rococo jugs rolled off shelves. He drew spirals with his fingers, paisleys in the deep undergrowth of hair. The water was warm, frothy in the shipboard sink, my hair swirling around his hands, like vines. Jacov hummed, serenading his own work. I must have drifted, supported on his palms, into a deep sleep, no longer alone, as I'd been in all the last traveling weeks. Under the cascading water of the sink, I dreamed of floral air, the primroses from the shady side of my father's garden, the twittering of squirrels and doves.

Years later, I still puzzled about the next sequence of events. I could never remember what transpired between the shampoo and the moment in the hairdresser's chair sitting before the mirror. There I was, upright, in the high-backed vinyl chair, my hair haloed over the top of my head, in huge pink curlers. My head weighted, slow in its turning, as if an icon in a procession. From my benign gaze into the mirror, I turned to the right, light glinting off the tight-pulled brown hair. I turned to the left, still in slow motion, tucking my chin, lowering my bedecked head slowly down from a level gaze, down the empty canvas of the mirror and into my own lap where Jacov, kneeling, had cradled his head. I saw his head, nestled between my legs. My black-and-white skirt was bunched up at my thighs; a crumpled wall of skirt obscured his face. My hands, I noticed, were gripping the chair. I saw my own legs, strong and tan, spread open on either side of him. And then, under the skirt, though his head barely moved, just a little, under my skirt, there was a wet licking. His long tongue was probing me. I felt hollowed out where he licked. His head seemed far below my conscious mind. As far away as the bottom of a chasm I had looked down into when I was a girl and hiking once in upstate New York. There too, my eyes shot down the dark walls to black water. There too, my feet seemed to be stretched inordinately, down to the cool bottom of the gorge, and my chest tall and dry atop a body distended, so the middle was only a wavery thin set of strands, and my long-ago feet, too far away to remember.

"Wait," I said, breaking the silence in the voice of a child. I heard my voice simply, in English, in the small room. Jacov lifted his face, softened, like plants underwater, drifty and open. "Wait. Wait . . ." I repeated.

When I slid off the chair, my skirt flipped down over my thighs with starched familiarity. At the door, turning the handle, I found it locked. Only then did panic begin. It started to circulate in swirls around my ankles and up my naked legs. Jacov took a single long stride to the door. He twisted the knob and opened it. It hadn't been locked.

I had taken a few slightly reeling steps down the corridor when Jacov called out. "Wait, don't go. I'll brush it out. You should not go like that. Let me finish your hair." He sounded so reasonable and professional that I felt chastised, silly, standing in the dark hall with my hair in curlers, my arms oddly akimbo. A pleasant midday light filled the salon through the porthole windows. Jacov stood calmly by the chair, waiting . . .

**1958**

# *pistachios*

All the early pictures of my mother are black and white, as if there really were no color then. I knew, dimly, about the trip to Cape Cod when my mother was sixteen. She'd told me, in one of her piecemeal stories, that she'd visited her cousin Belle in Provincetown on the Cape. I never met Belle but liked the name, and the familiarity with which my mother said the name, as though she didn't seem to notice that it was beautiful, that the word itself meant beauty. To her, Belle was just the name of her cousin. "Belle was there all summer, studying music. She was there with Ike, whom she later married. He got a Guggenheim. In art." I heard her pride, also the grammatically accurate and socially arrogant "whom."

Belle and her boyfriend, Ike, must have met her at the Provincetown wharf. Might they have been wearing hats? You saw hats in pictures from the late twenties. My own father wore hats. Maybe Ike's hat was straw, with a red feather upright; he was an artist. He'd have on white pants that would sound fresh and clean as they walked through the center of Provincetown, on Commercial Street. He'd carry Polina's case with ease. That would be unquestioned; a man, even a young man, even a young artist living in a common-law marriage, would carry the suitcase.

What if Belle wrapped a suntanned arm around that young Polina's waist and sashayed with her up the street? Belle's long gold hair would blow in Polina's face, the way my friend Deirdre's did, smelling new that peculiar way hair smells after a Breck shampoo. Not the way Polina's hair smelled, sort of stale. My mother had her hair done once a week, every week. By the end of the week it was tight, thick.

Maybe my mother, Polina, would have arrived at the Cape Cod wharf in 1928 with a bag of pistachios from Grand Central Station. It wasn't as if I had ever actually seen her eat pistachios. In fact, the only time I had seen them was that awful birthday party, my sixteenth, when she'd decided that I ought to have a "boy-girl party." She had planned everything. I was put at the head of the dining table, where my father usually sat, to preside over the formal dinner. My classmates, dressed up, were seated around the table.

"Shall I ring the bell for seconds?" My sister Joyce, at the foot of the table, played the role of our mother. She was stretching her legs under the table, knowing that when she touched the little mound that was the bell placed beneath the carpet and rang it for Elsie in the kitchen, the dinner party guests would be impressed. Elsie did come in and walked around the table, offering thin red slices of roast beef and then, in a second trip, Yorkshire pudding and mushy Brussels sprouts. I watched as Elsie made two complete rounds of the table with a dish in each hand. All the boys took meat. All the girls giggled. None of them had anything like this meal at home. They might have steak and mashed potatoes and probably always canned peas, if they had any vegetable at all. Joyce helped Elsie clear the plates, then brought in new salad plates. I didn't have to do any work, though I would have liked the excuse to leave the head of the table where I sat with a thin freezing smile. The kids took the salad politely, but none of them actually ate it. No one had a salad course in the fifties. The final humiliation, pistachio ice cream, had been chosen for dessert. It was like aquarium slime with sur-prise salty nuts, not chocolate chips in mint ice cream.

Our family had gone to Wellfleet for five years, before we girls were sent to camps so Polina and Leonard could travel. I had seen that very edge of Provincetown, its silvery dunes by the sea, where Polina said Belle's shack had been. Polina and Belle and Ike would have climbed to the top of a tufted dune. I knew the little hairs of grass that erupt from the sand on the dunes. The grass is perfectly green and so unscarred it doesn't seem real. Belle might have leaned on Ike's shoulder, the way Annette Funicello did in some episode I'd seen when the new TV was in the basement, when we were allowed to watch *The Mickey Mouse Club*. Belle would lean with a graceful hand on Ike's shoulder and slip off a leather sandal, because when you are on a dune, sand just gets trapped in shoes; it's better to take them off. Polina still had the leather san-dals that were made for her years before in Provincetown.

They laced up her tan legs all summer. We had been made to understand that these sandals were special, handmade to fit. They were "triple A, very, very, slim," like her feet, for which she had to buy expensive shoes, since the "ordinary ones just don't fit."

Polina, I imagined, would have sat down on a piece of driftwood or something, to unlace her city boots. Even then, when she was young, she couldn't have balanced on one foot. She would sit, as she did when she put on her ice skates at the Armory, where she insisted we go every Sunday. I'd watched her there, concentrating on lacing the skates as tight as possible, to show the line of her ankle, her tongue bulging in the corner of her mouth; a ritual of concentration I assumed was lifelong. If she had looked up between her left boot's unlacing, and her right, she'd have seen Ike holding Belle, one hand on each shoulder and kissing her. She might have dropped the boot in the sand.

No. She probably wouldn't have looked up. They probably wouldn't have kissed outside, in front of Polina. After all, "Belle was not married. Her mother, my aunt Minnie, was an anarchist."

Aunt Minnie herself had an illicit affair with one of her mother's brothers.

"Pressure was brought to bear," my mother said, somewhat obliquely, reporting on an event that predated her birth. The lovers were parted. The story of Minnie always ended with her return home to become Belle's mother. And so the story always seemed to fold in on itself; the passion that must have been there, evaporated with the proclamation

that "Minnie believed in free love." There were always unac-
countable holes in Polina's stories, but they were told with
such authority that I only slightly felt the icy air beneath.

My mother had been on her high school yearbook com-
mittee, on the debate team, and in the Anarchist Society, for
which she'd invited all candidates for office to come talk to
the club. "The communists, the socialists, the anarchists, all
of them. Once Earl Browder came to address our club," she'd
said. Long before I learned of his position in the American
Communist Party, I knew that the presence of this man con-
firmed that the Anarchist Society was something adults felt
they had to reckon with. Nothing in my life was like that.
None of my acquaintances ever talked about politics, none
started a society.

———

Probably it was on an autumn Saturday, when Polina had
decided to move all the family's wool clothes down from
their summer attic storage in mothballs, that she mentioned
another piece of the story. My father was away. He traveled
often then, to the West Coast, for film industry labor con-
ventions. Polina had been listening to the Saturday opera
on the radio, turned up dramatically loud, filling the whole
house. Weekends, especially when Leonard wasn't there,
were dedicated to Polina's projects. When Len was there,
the projects didn't go so well. When he was home, he just
wanted to relax, read the paper, have people over for drinks
or lunch. "Who's going to serve them, Len?" Polina would

demand. "I'm not going to be chief cook and bottle washer, goddammit!"

"No one is asking you!" he would roar back. It was like Olympian gods, huge, thunderous mountains. Neither would retreat.

But if he were there on a Sunday morning, my father would often get up early and take me with him to the deli. He'd stand in front of the rounded counter, his own belly growing more convex over the years, and point with a thick kind finger and delight in his voice. "How about a couple pounds of that lox? A dozen bagels. And let's have a quarter pound of that sturgeon for Mommy, eh?" He'd smile, lifting an eyebrow in mock quizzical gesture. I loved watching him survey the display. He seemed so comfortably pleased with the food.

Without him, the food looked repulsive. Wide trays stacked deep in pinkish salmon with yellowy strips. Dead heaps of smoked whitefish without heads, their scales a greenish gold. They were grabbed in the middle by the fat-handed guys in aprons behind the counter. Oily mackerel, dull, limp pickles. But with my father, the scene transformed to one of promise and delight. "Let's get a little coffee cake, too," he'd say, as if it were a novel idea. He'd pick out a poppy seed ring. It would be wrapped in a square white box with a skinny striped string tied in a bow.

By the time we got home, my sister, Joyce, would be in the kitchen following our mother's orders. She'd stand on a chair next to Polina, pulling apart the slices of lox and spreading them on one side of the platter. The slices would shred in her hands. Polina would bone the whitefish and break it into chunks. They'd both lick their fingers between fish pieces. "Cut a lemon," Polina would command. Or she would do it, cutting one into four irregular wedges, with the seeds half-cut or bulging so anyone squeezing a wedge would find lemon pits on their plate. I would set the table, trying to avoid being part of the now unappetizing display of salmon and whitefish.

Through the whole process, my father, who had brought the delicacies, would sit on his side of the table in the break-fast room reading the Sunday paper. Polina would call, "Girls, bring the orange juice." The order of events was unchanging and unquestioned. But why was it that everything had to be served, as if Polina were sitting at a restaurant? And why, I wondered, would she screech her chair back from the table when she finished a "course," and "clear" it all herself, in such a hurry?

The fall Saturday when Polina had announced that it was time for the shift of the clothes, Joyce and I were sent to carry armloads of clothes up and down. Our mother couldn't actually carry the clothes herself. Something about her back meant that she couldn't carry things and couldn't go on long drives, so that the family never went on family trips together, though all the rest of America seemed to be taking to the road. Even when we went to Cape Cod, Polina came by air-plane after Leonard had driven with us girls and the clothes and the sheets and towels for our vacation. He'd make a spe-cial trip back to an airport to pick her up. She would not have had to deal with Joyce throwing up somewhere near the tunnel into New York. She would not have had to deal with the stop at the Howard Johnson, where we would try to clean ourselves up in the bathroom. Nor would she be there to prevent the hamburgers and strawberry ice cream cones that our father would let us have.

But it was the opera that day that reminded her. "Have I ever told you about my aunt Minnie? Her daughter, Belle, could play the piano. She was almost as good as I was. Have I told you that I practiced six hours a day in high school?" She had indeed told us that, often. Our mother still played the piano sometimes, at night after we were supposed to be asleep. I could hear her manicured nails clicking on the ivory keys all the way up in my bedroom. The music was Chopin, the complicated trills coming in rushes and stops. She would work a problematic section over and over again. I never heard a piece played straight through. Did I just fall asleep, I'd wonder; or did Polina not care about the whole piece but only about fixing the problematic section? "Minnie was an anarchist," she would repeat, and I would nod dully, the smoke from Polina's cigarette thickening my brain. "You know," she added suddenly one time, "she was also a talented seamstress. She made clothes for Belle and me. She made me dresses and little bloomers to match so I could play on the swings when I was four and not have my underpants show." This was a new tidbit, the sewing as well as the competition, not to mention the dresses and bloomers and the notion of Polina remembering clothes she wore as a four-year-old. I'd noticed that if I just kept quiet, there would often be a new morsel. The danger was that Polina would interrupt herself with something like, "I'm not dead yet. You don't need to know all about my family."

"Oh!" I'd say, trying for the largest, most unobtrusive reaction so she wouldn't snap shut.

"Minnie and her husband fought all the time," she'd add, laughing affectionately. "They'd throw plates at each other." Why did the plates hurling through the air seem amusing? Minnie's fights sounded melodramatic, operatic. Polina and Leonard shouted at each other all the time, too, but their voices didn't soar; they shook the house, trembled the insides. "Minnie made clothes for Belle, but she didn't finish them. She finished mine," Polina would say, smugly, as if she had something on Belle. Then, "Neither Minnie nor Belle ever finished anything. They didn't have any discipline at all. Did I tell you about Ike's Guggenheim?" Polina would look accusingly, as if defying me to remember. I'd heard this part dozens of times and didn't really know what the point was, except that Ike's Guggenheim reflected well on my mother by association. The story always mentioned that Belle didn't "work" at her piano, Minnie didn't finish her brilliant sewing, and so both sank somehow into unremarkable old age as mere housewives. Even worse, "In the end, Minnie got real fat," the ultimate doom. Most of Polina's stories, if I could have articulated my own resistance to them, collapsed to anticlimax. There was a show of life, often glorious, reflecting somehow on Polina, and then the people just disappeared. Nothing ever added up to anything. All it ever came to was: "In the end . . ."

But here was Polina, standing in the hall, dressed in her slim soft khaki pedal pushers, her feet still in their Provincetown sandals, even though autumn was coming. At some level, it was clear that she was deeply dedicated to having kept going, to having become a doctor, and to having remained thin.

"Let's get going," she'd say, interrupting the brief rest between clothes trips. Back in the attic, I'd hoist another heavy mothball-scented set of woolens into my arms to take downstairs. Outside, the oak trees swayed grandly in the window. When I dumped the clothes onto one of the beds, inevitably, it seemed, because I didn't do it carefully, the heaviest coat would slide down and I had to disentangle it from Polina's Persian lamb coat, the one with small gray curls, and heave it back up to the bed. My life seemed so dreary.

# *dry ice*

Probably Leonard and Polina bought our house in Maryland because it accommodated parties. It was a showstopper. My elementary school friends asked if it was a mansion. It was true that the house was four stories high if you counted the large basement divided into rooms and an attic that was all rooms, as well as the ground floor and second floor. The rooms were pre–WWI large, and the house rose with a certain grandeur. The front entrance was on a busy street, one of the major east-west thruways. Because there was initially almost no sidewalk there, children usually entered through the back. That meant walking under a meandering wooden rose arbor with wild red roses, past gardens on both sides—the shade garden and the sun garden—quite different from most people's tidy postwar gardens. But it wasn't a mansion.

The first floor had four rooms: a living room, a kitchen, the sunroom, and a dining room with a bell under the table to summon servants. Also, there was a servant who answered the dining room bell. All the years that we were growing up, and even after we were grown and gone, there was a servant because Polina was a doctor. Nowadays, having a mother who is a doctor is unremarkable, but then, in the fifties, it was unknown.

Polina was a doctor and Leonard was a lawyer, and they were both pleased to have a large fine house and the where-withal to entertain. Their most casual annual event was the Fourth of July party, which was demanded by the location of the house, across the street from a country club that excluded Jews. Across the busy lane in front of the house was a large tract of land that had been designated hunt country at the turn of the century. Over time it had become a private club with a golf course, rolling hills, and tennis courts along the edge of the property across the street from our house. The tennis players frequently lobbed the balls over the tall wire fence, over the narrow lane, and into our front lawn. You could see the tennis balls wedged under the thick privet in the winter when the leaves were cleared. The balls were retrieved as hostages against exclusion, even though they were often dead by the time we extracted them. When Leonard and Polina learned that an annual fireworks event was held across the street at the country club, with extravagant displays of pyrotechnics, they invited everyone they knew who was in town in July. And just outside our hedge, the whole neighborhood lined up in folding chairs to watch the fireworks.

The party may have looked festive to the casual observer. Leonard, at the grill, made thick hamburgers and kosher hot dogs on the rolls that had been recently designed for the purpose. He'd figured out to grill the rolls, too, so they had nice black burn lines diagonally across. But, though it was the only day all year that we were allowed to have potato chips, I did not like the event at all. First of all, there was the hedge and all those people on the other side. Then there I was, in a little apron like Joyce's, walking around serving nuts and bringing tall drinks to the adults. I felt strange and separated from everyone else.

Polina was quite pleased the year when paper plates evolved and she could have a red, white, and blue ensemble of them. Every year she ordered little individual ice cream confections with flags on them from Clyde's Ice Creams. In the middle of the day before, Polina would drive to Clyde's to pick up the cartons of dessert that were hidden in a fog of dry ice. "Girls, do not touch the dry ice!" she'd warn ominously, with her cigarette dangling out of her mouth as she carried one steamy bag back into the house. My sister would be skipping up the path with a paper bag, blowing the steam with a serious expression. She was obviously excited about the party. I, last in line with the final bag, was distracted from the terror of dry ice by the exhilarating scent of the roses blooming on the arbor that stretched from the garage to the house. Inside their cartons, each ice cream was separated from the rest by a thin sheet of paper that we were to peel away from the flag without displacing it.

After the guests had eaten, Joyce and I would emerge with a paper plate and plastic fork in each hand to deliver the desserts before they melted. By the time we got ours, it would be growing dark and the adults would have moved their chairs to the front yard. I'd wolf down my ice cream, even though it always tasted faintly of cardboard.

The best moment of the July Fourth party was right before the fireworks when everyone, both inside and outside the privet hedge, was nestled in the chairs they had brought out front, lighting cigarettes, chatting quietly, intimately. Even the little children sitting in their parents' laps, scratching little patches of poison ivy or sucking their thumbs, were quieted before the explosions. Joyce would be with our parents' friends' kids, Corrie and her sister Pat, who were the same age as us.

It seemed as if Pat and Joyce were actually friends. From the time they were little, they would sit near each other with their heads close. I remembered passing them in the living room when they were five, playing with Ginny Dolls. Even their dolls had their heads together. I might have been envious but was too preoccupied with avoiding Corrie's contempt. Once when Corrie and I were seven, she'd challenged me "to poison your little sister Joyce." I didn't exactly know what poison was, but I had known not to put anything that wasn't food into my mouth. Nothing! "Take that thumb out of your mouth now!" Polina would hiss. I'd learned that lesson early and was continually astonished and annoyed that Joyce persisted. The method Corrie suggested, in the one activity in our lives on which and Corrie and I ever collaborated, was that I would slip wooden beads into Joyce's dinner. Joyce would eat them, and perish.

Trembling, I pushed the beads, an orange one into the rich meatloaf and a yellow, buttery one into the potatoes, my heart pounding. If I was brave enough to carry it through, I figured that Corrie might look at me with admiration instead of annoyance. Of course, Joyce just left the beads untouched on her plate.

At Corrie's house, in her commanding room on the third floor, Corrie made and broke rules. She'd listen at night, though she wasn't supposed to, to talk shows on her short-wave radio, stroking the smooth edge of her pillowcase. I, who spent the night in the trundle bed that fitted under Corrie's large double bed, was given a pillowcase without a special hem. However, if anyone had asked me, I would have said that Corrie was my friend, my best friend, my only friend. Leonard and Polina and Corrie's parents were friends. Joyce and Pat were friends. Corrie and I, the same age, were by definition friends.

At the July Fourth party, I'd use the excuse of Polina's commands—"Go get some ashtrays!"—to gallop away into the dark empty house, to root around in the living room by feel, gathering ashtrays. The lights had to stay off so the fireworks would show. It was still so soon after World War II that my elementary school had blackout shades in the class-rooms. Threat, though unmentioned, hovered. I felt as if I were on a private solitary mission and must trot silently and deftly through the house, prancing, like a colt.

The day after the party, my sister and I moved the chairs with their turquoise blue plastic webbing back to their exact spots in the backyard. Polina would gesture from the porch to the right or left if the chairs were off the mark.

Summer evenings returned to their usual routine. At dusk, we joined our parents with their martinis on the porch under the five hanging fuchsias, where they sat with a plate of brie and crackers to wait for Elsie to call us in to dine. We were careful to have only one or two crackers, like Polina, who slathered the brie half on, half dripping off a cracker. If we had more than that, Polina would say, "Now watch it, that has a lot of calories." I'd blush hot and want to spit the cheese out, but Joyce would lick the corners of her mouth, her long tongue curling around the edges. Our parents would be speaking in slightly inebriated voices. Polina would be telling Len that he looked "grossly overweight." My father would be smiling his most winning smile and teasing, "Now Polski, Polski, I don't think so," but his eyes would not be smiling. Polina might sort of shove him and say to me, "Run inside and see how long." Glad to leave, I'd go to the kitchen where Elsie sat on a stool, everything ready for dinner, just waiting for the exact time to deliver the meal.

"Mommy wants to know when dinner will be ready."

"Seven-oh-six," Elsie would reply, "just when she said. It will be ready at seven-oh-six, just like she said." We both understood that "she" meant Polina.

# *lip print*

In between getting married, an oft-repeated story itself, and settling down in Washington, Leonard went to war and returned. While he was gone, he sent letters back. I'd found some of the letters in an old file cabinet in the attic. I wasn't sure I wanted to see what they'd said to each other before I was born. But I needn't have been afraid. The letters were illegible. I could make out only a few words in some of Polina's letters, words like "had dinner with Sylvia and Gus," the same kind of factual reporting that was in her letters to me at camp. Leonard's letters were written in a small smudged script, much smaller than his writing as I knew it.

Often, Polina would say how poor they were then. She'd look at a dress she was considering buying for me from Garfinckel's—a dark blue dress, for instance, with finely stitched pleats and a crisp white collar, a dropped waist—and say that it cost as much as a week's worth of meals back then. If asked, I would not have known whether to take that as an accusation that the dress cost too much or a sideways boast that Polina could now afford such things. I couldn't believe, anyway, that my parents had ever really been poor.

I knew that Polina and Leonard dined at the Sleek Fox. The Sleek Fox featured a fox slinking minimally across the menu, just the outline of one. When I was ten, we were taken there. Up to that point, the most extravagant restaurant I'd been in was a local Chinese place called the Peking Palace, which featured little-girl cocktails with small parasols and wonton soup that we tried to eat with chopsticks. The benches were red plastic that got more worn each year when we came for my birthday dinner.

The Sleek Fox was a silver-lined den, the walls gray, the tables low, the music live. The pianist nodded in recognition of our parents when they entered and segued to their song, "The September Song." Polina wore jewelry, gold globs in her ears. Leonard wore the requisite white shirt, gleaming like his teeth. They were debonair, de rigueur. Polina had her usual cigarette with her martini. She had learned to smoke in Scotland. In the dim light of the restaurant, I looked at the package of Chesterfields with new admiration. I noticed the gold emblem on the cover, its Eiffel Tower–like construction, perfect on the white background, part cathedral, part escutcheon, referring to the crowned heads of Europe. My mother had a cigarette case made of light brown leather. It was well tanned, supple, smooth, and obedient to her distracted shoves. For instance, while driving to Garfinckel's on a Saturday morning to get clothes for one or the other of us, the Chesterfield package could be scrunched smoothly into the case, without her really taking her eyes off the road.

After dinner, Polina would apply her lipstick without the mirror. She blotted it with a Kleenex. There were lip prints on the pieces of Kleenex in her purses. There were tiny flakes of tobacco in the corners of her purses where the leather seams were. I knew that from times Polina asked me to "run upstairs and check" one or another purse for her car keys. The cigarettes in the ashtray at the Sleek Fox all had a faint outline of lipstick on them—like glamorous kisses. I hardly said a word during dinner but had entertained myself watching my parents, watching the musician with his shiny head and meandering tunes. Polina ordered a chocolate mousse for dessert. Leonard made his joke about Polina being able to eat anything and not gain weight. I watched my mother have about a third of the "scrumptious" dessert and leave the spoon awkwardly jammed into the remaining slightly melting pile. I did not expect that I would ever have a song with someone, or that a pianist would play it when I entered a room.

## *sex ed*

I learned about Polina's first husband when I was twelve. The story came about in such a detached manner, with so little connection to anything familiar, that I absorbed mostly the importance of not telling my sister. My mother had called me into her study, a small room where she kept her medical books, her opera records, and the household bills. I didn't know why I'd been called in. Polina had a legal pad with yellow lined pages and sat in front of me as if the study were a small seminar room.

"I am going to show you where babies come from," she announced, quite out of context. It was 6 p.m., an hour before dinner.

I'd been in my room, reading something for history class about the Roman Empire and doodling at the desk facing the western sunset. I was feeling hungry, but since Polina was home early and Elsie was cooking, I couldn't go into the kitchen. My eyes kept drooping; my left hand kept moving up to my ponytail and, instead of taking notes, trying (mostly in vain) to move through my hair without getting snagged in knots. When it came to a tangle, my hand wriggled gently to loosen it. The challenge was to see how long I could remain patient. Not very long. Soon I'd have yanked the rubber band out of my hair in disgust and grabbed a brush. Then, with every obstructed stroke, I would move closer to fury, to hurling the hairbrush across the room and roaring, silently, my throat raw with self-hatred.

But I only had my hand in the ponytail, phase one, when Polina, after a single rap at the door, opened it to my surprise and said, "Come to my study. I need to talk to you." The request certainly woke me up. I was nervous and curious.

Polina had already drawn the anatomy of the lower half of the female body in thick lead strokes. I had never seen my mother draw anything, not ever. So it was striking just to see the lines. I couldn't even tell what it was, since there was no head and no feet.

"Here is where the eggs are made," Polina said, demonstrating the location on the yellow pad with the rounded point of the pencil. "If they are not fertilized by the daddy, they are thrown away." I didn't have any idea what Polina was talking about. I didn't understand what fertilizing could have to do with whatever she was explaining, since my association with fertilizing was so literal. In the fall, my father would take out the rusty fertilizer spreader and fill it with a sweet-smelling white powder that he sifted over the lawn.

"The lawn needs to eat; it's hungry," he'd say. "We have to find a day between rains. There needs to be rain, or the fertilizer will burn the grass," he'd explain. Fertilizer, for the lawn at least, seemed paradoxically a dangerous and crucial addition. But I knew enough not to interrupt Polina's explanation. I got the part about the eggs traveling down the fallopian tubes, because Polina had drawn them descending. I didn't understand how eggs turned to blood, well, not blood, Polina had called it something else. I thought that maybe it was like the inside of cracked eggs. I was sitting on the hassock watching, trying not to move. I thought that if I moved Polina might tell me to "stop fidgeting." I probably had a stupid expression.

Polina had closed the door of the study, making this an unusual private meeting. A privilege, even one I didn't understand, was not to be squandered. When Polina concluded that the process with the unfertilized eggs led to "menstruation," I was aghast at her mouthing of that word. No one called it that. "Men-stru-a-tion," Polina continued, "is *not* a sickness. Do you understand? It is perfectly natural." I was aware that she was trying to contradict someone. "Elsie told me you had been sick a few weeks ago, and you were not sick," Polina insisted.

"I know, I never thought I was."

In the quiet of the den, Polina closed the legal pad and took a Chesterfield out of the pack. She inhaled deeply. There was still a smoldering cigarette in her ashtray. She had stubbed it when she started the lecture, but not snuffed it. I watched the smoke, eyes downcast, in a combination of calm and agitation. I couldn't imagine what was coming. Was my mother going to tell me about sex? I didn't exactly know what was involved with sex but had just read *Othello* in Mr. Lapin's class. I loved the idea of a "beast with two backs." I loved the idea of Mr. Lapin. He had aquatic eyes, green and quick. He had a slim body. He was an actor; he did Gilbert and Sullivan in the summer. I'd seen him strike his lovely thespian poses, his slim body arching toward a raised hand, his agile voice rippling over complicated lines. He thought I was brilliant at reading Shakespeare. It was the first time I'd ever even been noticed in a class. Polina and Leonard had given him their blessing because they knew his parents, who were doctors, and had met his wife. At the end of the year, he'd given me a book of Shakespeare inscribed "To My Best Student."

Polina must have mistaken my stillness for rapt attention. But it wasn't. It was more like conjuring, trying to bring up the sylvan green of language, of Mr. Lapin, of moonscape and mystery into this room thick with smoke and ugly words.

"Dear . . ." Polina was saying in a new voice, a voice that said she was going to address me in some new way. I held my breath, not wanting to hear my mother talk about penises. But she didn't.

"I was married once before Daddy. I was very young. My father saw the man kiss me and insisted that I marry him if I wanted to go back to school in Scotland. I knew it wasn't right." Polina puffed on her cigarette.

"On our way to getting married, I made him agree that if it didn't work out, we'd divorce."

I didn't know where to begin. Nor, in a way, was there any need to begin. It was all done, sewn up, dismissed. There seemed no particular lesson to be gleaned, not like the distinct notion that to have your period was not to be sick—a confusion I hadn't even had. Just a capsule of events delivered like a pill.

"OK," I said, hoping that was the right answer.

"You are not to tell Joyce, she's still too young."

"OK," I said again, slightly more solemnly, willing to protect the secret entrusted to me in my new mature state, superior to my sister, though unsure what about it required age.

"Who was he?" I asked tentatively.

My mother seemed surprised at the question. "Alfred was a medical student too, but in research. He liked fishing," she said, inconclusively.

Though I didn't examine it, I had a tangled version of Alfred as a fisherman and my mother as lure, as if Polina had been fly-fishing bait. Her hair would have been thick, dark, gleaming with health—like the fur of the muskrat or an American grizzly, from having licked fish oil, something with which to catch something. I didn't dwell on what was being caught. Her mouth, in bright cherry lipstick then, like the cherry of the gigantic bush at Alfred's English grandmother's farm, which would have flowered in spring and be full of big juicy berries in summer. I couldn't remember whether Alfred was supposed to be English or American, and I almost completely forgot he was studying medicine. The fishing part seemed more vivid. Her limbs would have looked long and white, clearly of a sandpiper, hinged stiff. In every picture after her high school ones, Polina wore high heels. She wore straight skirts and stockings, with tailored blouses, and walked with great authority. Polina would not have noticed Alfred, beyond his usefulness as a person to dine with after classes at St. Andrews. He took her to restaurants she wouldn't have treated herself to. She had told me this part. I, who of course didn't have a boyfriend, wondered what it would be like to have so many men interested that you wouldn't notice them.

I didn't even think it was like Frank, the boy in my class who had come over one summer day, uninvited. I hadn't ever noticed him in class and didn't know why he was there, suddenly, in July, when I was in my usual summer miasma, nothing to do but endure the thick humidity and the endless dizzying hum of insects. Frank had kissed me, right outside, at the back door. It felt like a large flabby toad had been smeared on my mouth (if toads were ever flabby). I had to resist spitting afterward. I'd drawn back in disgust and realized that Frank thought I was being demure.

My mother said that Alfred came to visit when she was home, in New Jersey, one summer, between her second and third year at university in Scotland.

"I was playing the piano in the parlor," she said.

I remember being startled by the parlor. What did she mean? Was it really a parlor, a special room, like with wallpaper of silver birds and Polina at a mahogany piano? Or was that just an old word for the place the upright piano was? Anyway, Saul entered the parlor and discovered his only daughter, her dark hair, maybe, in disarray, her lipstick smudged, and Alfred gaping by her on the bench. Alfred probably leapt to his feet. It was difficult for me to decide whether to imagine the characters in my mother's stories having polite diffidence or embodying the savoir faire of Edith Piaf, a favorite of hers.

"You will marry that young man or you will not return to Scotland," Saul decreed, according to Polina, who quoted him when she told the story.

"He gave me an ultimatum. I wasn't going to not return to Scotland," Polina said, in an uncharacteristic double negative. "But I had misgivings from the start. On the way to the wedding, even before we got married, I got Alfred to agree that if it didn't work out, we'd split up, no questions asked," she repeated.

Obviously, Polina was proud to have got it right, to have dealt with an impossible situation with such foresight.

## to keep from scratching

Polina had been holed up in her bedsit on Prince Street, not far from St. Andrews University, Scotland, for three whole days before her landlady called a doctor. I knew this story because I'd been told how "idiotic" the landlady was. The landlady probably carried thin beef consommé and saltines up to Polina's room. Or that was what I imagined. When I was sick, that was what Polina did. She brought consommé. She'd say, "Here's your lunch. Drink lots of liquids." I suspected that no one I knew at school had ever seen consommé. I was always startled by the sad taste of it. It made me want to get well, to eat something I could actually chew. Being sick seemed so lonesome, so empty, so like the thin soup with nothing in it.

Polina had talked about the month she spent in a Fevers Hospital, when she was at university. She'd planned a trip with one of her brothers and her grandfather, Philip, through the Ukraine, but she "fell ill." Her apparent cold turned out to be scarlet fever, and she was quarantined for a month. I was seven or eight when I first heard the story. It was the long, long time Polina was to have remained alone in a room by herself that impressed me first. "I was a grown-up," Polina would add, "but they had nowhere else to put me except the Children's Fevers Hospital. They wouldn't put me in with a bunch of children, so they put me in a ward by myself." Watching her righteous face as she spoke, I absorbed, without question, my mother's superiority to the children, the bunch of them. I tried to see her as she'd been then. I imagined that there would be a thrush outside Polina's window but that she would not notice. A thrush, even the word *thrush*, which I knew was some sickness horses got, captivated me. But Polina, able to lie a whole month alone in a ward, Polina able to remain focused on whatever she undertook, not only not distracted but not noticing anything else, Polina would not hear the thrush pecking at the screen, if they even had screens in Scotland when Polina went to university there.

When I'd heard that the landlady thought Polina had a cold at first, I presumed she must have brought a vaporizer, one of those upside-down brown bottles that made steam. That's what I had when I had a cold, when I was little. That's probably what she had when she got scarlet fever.

Oddly enough, I also had scarlet fever, when I was three. But by then antibiotics were used. There is a picture of me, sitting up in a little child's bed with a quilt. The picture, taken in 1949, is black and white, but I remembered that the quilt was a pale satiny pink. I am leaning forward on the bed with a wise little smile on my face. The little girl in the picture had soft brown curly hair. She looked sweet that way. I couldn't imagine myself as that person. But I could remember breathing in, with those vaporizers, how the air was forced into the narrow channel still open. I remembered the two decongesting vaporizers that bubbled cozily all night. In the whole moist universe of that room, I was a misted sleeping plant.

When Polina had been ill, it must have been spring, because she was planning to go on summer holiday. The exams for the term would be over. Polina had finished her first and last term as a literature student. She had not told her family in America about her shift in plans, her intention to become a doctor. Polina had spoken of her victory over her family. She told us that she'd gone to Scotland, not America, for two reasons. First, she'd gotten a C on an English paper at NYU. "Not because it wasn't well written," she would insist, "but because of the topic. I wrote about Sacco and Vanzetti. I was there, in Union Square with my anarchist cousin, and the teacher didn't approve of my politics." (It was assumed that somehow we understood what it meant to be "there in Union Square.")

"I decided then and there that I would not stay where they didn't grade on a fair basis!" Then, on the lookout for alternative schools, Polina had somehow heard about St. Andrews from some friend of a cousin probably; I imagined a friend of Belle's. "I heard they didn't have a Jewish quota there," Polina explained with no hint of self-pity. A solution to a problem she hadn't even mentioned before, as though it were obvious. "I took a year of English and then a required psychology course. What outraged me was why they didn't consider anatomy in the psych course. How could they not know how the brain works? It was absurd. Ridiculous!" At this point I always winced. I wasn't sure why it was "absurd." It seemed possible, to me, to speak of the mind and the emotions without the body. That's certainly how it felt to me, separate.

"I went to the head guy. He was a dean and had a nice smile. He said, 'Polina, sounds like you'd like to be a physician.' I told him that's what I wanted, but my parents were afraid to have a girl be a doctor. I had an uncle who was a doctor who died of TB. 'Polina,' he said, 'why don't you just start the program? We just shan't tell your parents for a while, shall we?'"

That was it, the whole story as we ever heard it, told in an attempted Scottish accent for the dean's lines. Polina always looked so happy when she said what the dean had said. Had no one ever made a little conspiratorial plan with her? She looked so special, so chosen.

———

The scarlet fever had happened between that first year in school and her new life as a medical student. Once, I was alone in the house with her when she was coming down with stomach flu. She had undressed, laying her clothes on the chaise lounge in her bedroom. "Ooh! Ooh!" she wailed. "Goddammit!" She told me to get a nightgown out of a drawer. I chose the one at the top of the pile, a neatly ironed creamy satin, my hands trembling at my mother's furious pain. "Not that one. The green one!" Then she slept.

I kept coming to the door, only to see her still in bed, still asleep, snoring. Her thin face quivered with each exhalation. Her head was turned away from the window. I remembered that, since I would have faced the window, hoping for a sliver of sunlight. Only in the late afternoon, when the sun had moved out of range and the room darkened in shadow, did Polina's eyelids begin to flicker and then her eyes to open, to stare fixated. It was frightening to see her, so distantly detached.

Polina's pink bed jacket would have been hooked over the shoulder of her desk chair. It would have rippled in silken softness, moving as the air wafted through it. I was sure about the bed jacket. Polina still had bed jackets, a whole collection of them with lace and little strings to tie them. Perhaps her head had been damp as she slept. Little drips of heat from the fever would have lined her forehead. Wait, she didn't perspire. She complained in the summer, when she played tennis, that she couldn't sweat. She'd just turn red and apply damp cloths to her face so natural evaporation would cool her. This phenomenon had always seemed enviable. I sweated so copiously in high school that I brought a cardigan every day to cover the damp patches under my arms, even though the cardigan made it worse.

Her mouth might have been open and red inside when she had scarlet fever, the way it was sometimes when I'd come into my parents' bedroom when I was little and frightened. I'd see Polina, on the other side of the bed, her form lank and limp under the sheets, her mouth dangerous-looking. I'd crawl in next to Leonard, who usually cracked open an eye and smiled sleepily. But I stopped coming after the time my father hadn't woken up but had punched me in his sleep. Waking, he was apologetic, but it was a scary moment, not worth the possible comfort of being in there with them.

The cracker would be wet where the consommé would have spilled when the tray was put down at lunchtime. Polina wouldn't have touched it. Often she wouldn't touch things. I always ate what was put in front of me. Polina used to brag to people that her children were not spoiled about eating, that we didn't have "silly phobias."

Polina only mentioned her scarlet fever to get to the part about knitting. To keep her from scratching the intense itch, the nurses taught her how to knit. Intuitively, I understood, though it didn't really make sense. How would knitting make you stop scratching? Polina had to have her fingers engaged, doing something. That's what the knitting must have done; that's what her smoking, her lighting and holding and putting out the cigarettes, must have done, prevented her from some self-harm.

I knew about itching, not from having scarlet fever but from getting poison ivy. I'd lived for the exquisite pleasure of the mildest contact with anything, a sheet accidentally sliding along the raised welts. In the hospital bed, Polina, like me, might have dreamed she was rubbing her hands back and forth over some dry twigs. Her claws would rake deep lines in the dry clotted soil and dig for the moist bog beneath. She might dream she heard the howling of some agonized hound, then wake to discover it was herself, scratching in her sleep. In Polina's case, the nurses walking through the ward would have seen her. The nurses were used to children. After all, it was a hospital for childhood fevers. Usually, Polina told me, they could sedate the children for the duration of the itching with tiny drops of belladonna. They'd administered a child-sized dose to Polina. Her pulse leapt, her heart began to fibrillate. It is well-known in the family that Polina, and somehow therefore I as well, was sensitive to drugs. This little dose almost did Polina in. The nurses had had to give her digitalis to revive her. That must have been when they decided on the more mechanistic approach of knitting. First, they slathered "oxide of zinc" all over her.

"Calamine lotion," Polina would say, translating for her daughters, uncharacteristically, to something familiar.

That detail of the story was understandable. Once, when I was about eight and had a really bad case of poison ivy, our parents had been out of the country. It was a hot September weekend day, and Elsie had decided to take us to the air-conditioned movies. The movie was *Gone with the Wind*. So there we sat, Joyce on one side, Elsie—a large Black woman with a bowl of calamine lotion in her lap—in the middle, me on the other side. I watched the movie through a screen of tears, interrupted every so often by Elsie leaning over to dab pink calamine on my arms, which I must have been rubbing. The irony of the scene was apparent to neither of us girls. We emerged from the wonderfully chilly movie theater, all three, with teary red eyes. My skin was a flaky pink from dried layers of lotion.

"No one was allowed to touch me or the wool, since I was infected. So when I got stuck . . ." I always noticed the way

Polina landed on *p*'s and *k*'s. I could hear the phlegm click in back of Polina's throat when she said "stuck." Maybe no one else noticed, but it was embarrassing, too overtly physical, something my friends' mothers would have the manners not to display. "I'd put the wool on the rolling bed tray, and a nurse would roll it to an expert in the next room. Then they rolled it back, with instructions." This was the kind of communication Polina liked, I realized; only the relevant information and written on a sheet of square lined paper. Like when she departed for the hospital in the morning and left the menu written out for Elsie and the shopping list for Elsie to call in. Even as a medical student, Polina must have liked all those people waiting on her.

# best friend

Though I might have said that my father was my best
friend growing up, it wasn't as if we spoke much to one
another. Most of my best experiences with him were non-
verbal. Joyce had a whole different way of being with him.
Even when she was little, she stood up to him on her two
sturdy legs, her little eyebrows furrowed, just like his. By the
time she was a teenager, my sister was arguing vigorously,
to no effect, with Leonard. Not me. With my father, it was
as if he'd come with me, even just a little way, into some
domain that was not controlled by anyone, that just existed.
For instance, in the summer, both of us would notice the
gigantic bumblebees that would avoid the pale pink azalea
with the languorous blossoms in favor of the deep Florida
pink one with its tightly curled perky buds. In the garden, he
taught me about worms; we both smiled when we found one.
We would motion each other to the window for a sunset.
One winter night after a snow, the two of us stood outside

under a large pine where a streetlight illuminated the gigantic flakes that drifted down. The shadow of the pine etched precisely on the snow.

I found a photo of Leonard, standing alone in a white suit, looking out over some harbor somewhere, and took it up to my room. Sometimes, I cut a single rose and put it in a small vase near his desk, in mute appreciation.

Deirdre came along in fourth grade. She had wide-apart blue eyes, thin lips, and a pale hand that was covered in light down. She looked a little like Mary Martin playing Peter Pan, with boyish hips and a pleasant puckish face with eyes that slanted up. She had been adopted by a tall woman with gray hair hanging down the sides of her head. In their backyard were pansies. Pictures of Deirdre, surrounded by heart-shaped haloes, with her name embossed on almost everything in the house, meant that she was the treasure of her parents.

Deirdre seemed quite detached from her odd, older parents, and they seemed to dote on her. It was the reverse of what I knew. Deirdre's mother was always around when we came home after elementary school. She made chocolate chip cookies for us. Sometimes she even gave us milk and sandwiches, thick creamy peanut butter in two clouds of white bread, as a snack, defying all the rules of our house.

At night, at Deirdre's house, when her father was who knows where, maybe white-haired and silent in his study, staring at the heart-shaped pictures, she would run upstairs ahead of me and turn out all the lights. Deirdre would hide always in a new place, waiting for me to come up, one tentative foot at a time. Was she in a closet or under a sofa or behind a door with her pointed ears and her diabolical laugh? None of these places were visible from the staircase.

"Ha!" Deirdre would shriek.

I'd grin a cold grin above my pounding heart.

# beaux

The last year of Polina's studies involved a rotation in obstetrics, which took place in Dublin. Alfred remained in Edinburgh. In retrospect, I realized that Polina would have worn no jewelry in the delivery room in Dublin, no wedding ring. Did Polina tell me about the man she met in Dublin when she was putting on the white ball gown to go to a party with Leonard? That was the same dress she wore in one of the full-length portrait photographs she had of herself. It was white gauze, strapless, so the white folds were elegantly wrapped around her bodice. The gown was a floor-length fountain that flowed down in an architecturally clean line. Polina had gorgeous high heels, also white, that showed under the dress. In the photograph, which was a formal picture from Brooks Portraits, Polina was seated, gazing, so her neck was long, over her right shoulder at the camera. Her hands were placed gently one above the other on her lap in a completely uncharacteristic way. Her face was soft in a gentle smile I had never seen.

"I was quite the belle of the ball when I was in Scotland," Polina would say. "There was an Indian resident who was rich. He wanted to have me visit him."

I never found out what happened with the Indian doctor, since the story usually morphed into a tale about another wealthy boy who'd been interested in Polina when she was in high school.

"He'd come by chauffeur to visit me. One time, though, he was sick, and I went over to his house to bring him his homework. His mother treated me so badly I dropped him."

I'd not known what to say to this revelation. It seemed too scary to ask what had happened with the mother.

There was also a Canadian medical student in Dublin, whose father was Jewish and whose mother was Catholic. Those were the first aspects of him that Polina mentioned. They seemed the usual non sequitur at first, but turned out somehow to be pivotal. "I fell for him," was how Polina usually put it, "but then he had to go back home to take care of his mother and sisters. His father had died." I wondered what Polina falling for someone had been like. Her story left the impression that it was because his mother was Catholic, because there were so many girls, so many children, that he left. There was a hint of disdain when she said, "He had to take care of his mother." I understood that no one had "taken care of" Polina; she'd made her way on her own and expected no less from anyone else. Maybe the man was susceptible to guilt, to a false sense of duty, or maybe the family was help-less without their remaining male. Either way, it didn't reflect well on the guy. Polina never explained.

She'd speak at some other time about saying goodbye at a train in a downpour, always mentioning that she was wear-ing her trench coat in this scene and that she got drenched. By then, I'd seen *Casablanca*.

**1960**

# Passover

I t's late! Get up, girls." Polina clapped her hands sharply from her bedroom across the hall. My eyes snapped open. I smelled her woozy Chesterfield smoke seeping under the door. I recalled the weight of the day, Passover. On the third floor, Joyce slept. At the head of the double bed Polina was probably sitting upright, flicking her index finger, seeing her nail polish chipped already. The problem was in going to the salon the day before, instead of today.

"Leonard," she'd say, nudging him, "get up. The liquor guy will be here in twenty minutes. Hurry!" Polina would mash her cigarette into the bedside ashtray and dress quickly. Leonard moved off the bed and into the bathroom.

"Polski," he called from there, "the Rosenbergs will probably send flowers again. Do you care where they go?"

"Yes! Of course I do," Polina said, standing in the doorway, tiny loaves of guest towels from the hall linen closet balanced in each hand. "Just don't put them in the blue Yugoslavian vase, it's too jammed with all those flowers. Look, you take care of it, Len. Please! I have a thousand other things. And don't forget we have a tennis court at eleven."

Downstairs, the front door bell did not chime but rasped like an industrial buzzer. I, still in bed, shuddered at its insistence.

"There's the liquor guy at the door now, Leonard," I heard my mother call into the bathroom. "Hurry up, you know how much time he takes."

———

By the time Polina came down the gracious sweep of stairs to the breakfast room off the kitchen where Elsie was working, Elsie had already directed the deliveries to the sunroom.

In the breakfast room, Polina sawed at her boiled egg-shell with a blunt knife, in the manner she learned in medical school, in Scotland. "Elsie, be sure you put the chicken livers in with the other party stuff, in the second fridge. Elsie!" Polina's voice was strident. "Get me some *hot* coffee."

I imagined Leonard fifty years ago, on Pesach, standing in a dirt street in a Polish town, his father shouting to the tawny houses with small closed-in windows, listening for the answering call of an uncle, "Yacob! Yacob!" His father's voice soared into the quiet. A gray-bearded figure in a doorway asking, "Moishe?" tentative but growing more hopeful as the man walked stiffly toward them. Then, lost in tears and murmuring, the man would embrace his nephew, Leonard, his short black American hair a defiance, as he stared at this great-uncle's face, damp with tears on papery white skin.

"Leonard?" Polina's voice shot up the stairs the next time the buzzer sounded.

"Tell Mr. Jaeger to come up," Leonard called back, pulling up a second sock. "We can talk about the wine up here."

Joyce had arrived at the breakfast table in pajamas and a robe. Her long hair was in its nighttime braid. Her face was an elongated version of Leonard's. Each had a square jaw, a straight nose, and agile eyebrows. Hers seemed permanently drawn into an arrow of interrogation. The severe left eyebrow pulled down toward her nose was so distracting that one could miss the bottomless brown of her eyes. Accepting the orange juice glass from Elsie, Joyce licked the night off her teeth.

"Can I have that section?" She pointed to the front page of the *Washington Post* with the combativeness of a political science major, though now, at fourteen, she was thinking of cultural anthropology.

"What do you want me to do today?" she asked, resigned to hearing the instructions. She just had to get through the weekend, then she'd go back to her real life in high school.

"Don't bother me now, Joyce," said Polina, who left with the City section of the paper for the small downstairs bathroom, one of her morning rituals.

"Where is she?" I exhaled in relief when I met only my sister in the breakfast room. Joyce gestured with her whole hand toward the hall bathroom, her mouth full of toast. I was already tall, shapely in an old-fashioned way at sixteen.

Riding lessons and ice-skating classes had given my thighs curve and my calves strength. My hair curled in a jumble and fell around my face without any attention. My eyes were a muted green, and the rest of my face was still thick with childhood cheeks and shy wide lips. I didn't know what I wanted for breakfast, maybe an egg like my mother's, but not so watery; maybe toast, like Joyce, who always seemed more up on things. She knew the latest hairstyles, the right food to eat. Her broad white teeth crunched into her browned bread without a second thought. I eyed Polina's place at the table. She had eaten some of her egg, the rest had dripped, the yolk stiffened on the edge of her eggcup from Quimper. Yellow, thick over the white cap of the French maiden in her crinolines on the cup. Polina's toast crust had lipstick on it. She'd only had a bite or two, and marmalade was spread haphazardly on the piece that remained, with large dry patches between the thick orange mounds.

"Look, girls." Polina spoke as she strode back into the breakfast room. I chafed under that blanket of "girls" thrown over my shoulders. "Girls," the way the word sidled up, condemning us to obedience. "Look, girls, you need to be available today. Don't go running off all over the place, your father needs help with chairs and things, please."

Where would we go running anyway? I wondered.

Later, Elsie accompanied Polina to the sunroom to view the table, the creamy cloth, the flowers, the wine glasses sparkling with sunshine. Polina saw the scene as separated colored points of shape, quickly accessed. "Elsie, you forgot the silver salt shakers, they need to be polished, too."

Leonard also surveyed the scene, dwelling an instant on the yellow tulips. He would have enjoyed red more. He saw the scowl on his wife's brow.

I hovered by the French doors. The flowers attracted me, the tiny purple irises, dancing baby's breath, blue anemones, and peppermint carnations amid the yellow tulips, flanked by wine goblets and the glinting silver candlesticks from Copenhagen.

The year before, I'd been allowed to invite Mr. Lapin to Pesach. I'd watched him all evening. I'd watched especially how he had sliced his gefilte fish, his fine lean jaw quiet, his agile fingers deft. Did anyone ever slice it in my family?

# downstairs, upstairs

The evening streetlights were almost on. The air was soft to summon spring. In the kitchen, Elsie's uniform was white, stretched over her hard round belly. She moved fast, an umbrella shape on spindly heels. Her hands exchanged cooked for uncooked trays of tiny livers perched on perfect discs of water chestnuts. She shafted small nutted cheese balls through their globular middles to attach them to the rounds of toast they rested on. Elsie knew where the silverware was, where the candles hid with crumbs, in corners in the large house. She knew how to tie an apron, how to smile at white-skinned babies born to parents with swimming pools, with their light yellow ringlets and red party dresses. She knew how to watch the daughters, now grown up, skim through the kitchen, laying claim to the celery in the refrigerator, to the regular glasses not for guests. Where did she go at night?

Here she was when the curtain was lifted, talking to her Black coworkers in the sunroom, their sweating heads bowed in glassed-in subservience. Hidden deep was anger, as they observed with intrigue, delight, and contempt the many-layered white world. The two Black men, Ernest and Alvin, Elsie's in-laws, were dressed as butlers. Their every move was choreographed by long cooperation. In and out. Ice in buckets. Napkins in piles. Glasses in rows. Toothpicks in tumbling hills. Smiles not yet attached.

Upstairs, Joyce and I were each inspecting our own faces up close to the mirror in my room. *Look at her velvet eyes*, I thought enviously. She was sticking pins in her hair to raise it high like Nefertiti's.

"My hair looks awful," I said, fury and self-disgust swirling. I'd have thrown the hairbrush across the room if I'd had it in hand.

"Here, I'll put a pin in," Joyce said, kindly.

Polina in her bedroom had set to work dressing herself. The neckline of her white, jeweled dress ended in a sharp point. Gold bracelets encircled her long arms, and on her finger, the aquamarine ring. Her hair had turned out all right. She dabbed a quick perfume, heavy, extravagant. She left, shutting the door with a bang. Polina peered in on her daughters, focused on the wisps of Joyce's hair that had burst out of her French twist and the naked width of my neck.

"Here, dear, wear this," she said, offering a heavy leafed Grecian necklace for the evening. I sagged under its thick bronze weight. I couldn't tell if I hated it because it was ugly, or because it was so distinctly my mother's. Was I meant to grow into loving it?

# "the silent person"

From my position across from my sister in the middle of the long table, I could see our mother perched at one end. The two of us had the only silver goblets. We faced one another, divided by the huge bouquet. I sat stiff, leaning a little forward. The ice cubes, the silverware, the anticipation of the fifteen guests were all shimmering. Polina put a thin Spanish lace scarf on her head. It rested on her head crookedly. She began to say the words to the first blessing. Every year she asked questions about one or two of the words. When she read them she usually, with a great forcing sound, got the one she worked on right, while all the others around it faltered.

"'Ha O'lam' like this, Mommy," I'd said, "Ha means *the*, *O'lam, world. Blessed art thou, King of the world.*" I'd tried by dint of the majesty of the meaning to force her into the proper intonation. She always laughed.

"*Baruch Atah Adonai,*" she recited, her head moving up and down to the words as though she could bob them out of her.

"*Blessed art thou,*" the chorus intoned. Polina removed the scarf as all the eyes looked elsewhere.

Completely embarrassed, under the table my thighs pressed against the chair. I imagined their girth. *All the lights are shining on me,* I thought, mortified by the one bulb that was indeed over my head, though not particularly bright. Oh for a pulsing feathered bird to thunder itself up to me in the gargantuan night, its heavy wings spread hugely over my bed. I wished something Shakespearean would take me somewhere where I'd be beautiful.

———

In the ceremony, the leader of the Seder condemns the wicked child, who separates herself from the others, disdaining to be counted as one among them. Wickedness, though, was not exactly how I experienced it. More untouchable, or shadow. I remembered a time when there was no separation. Some summer when the family had been at Cape Cod, I was playing in one of the freshwater ponds we'd stop at on the way home from the beach to get the sand off. In the water I alone rolled over and over and over like a log. Over and over, so that up and down disappeared. My hair followed me around in the water, drifting, long and brown before my eyes, as I rolled round and round, knowing that I and the shafts of light were floating specks in the same substance.

But then, walking from school my first day, in a green kilt—walking up the half block from school through the brassy autumn trees, scuffing the leaves—somehow the transition occurred. I became aware that my mouth was too big, felt my arms awkward in a navy blue sweater. I had seen that the other girls and boys had sweaters with holly trees dancing on them, tiny flowers, cuffs folded along some invisible line that matched the neat cuffs of their clean white socks. Their hair was ribboned and glistening. How, in that short stretch of the world between the public school and our large white house, up the pleasant curve of sidewalk with pine trees and grass, the neighbor's hump of pinkly flowered bush, the heady drone of honey bees, the white clouds and the birds, how in that little space of territory had a shadow come down and attached itself to my form? All my clothes and my sandwiches and my crayons and the way I would learn to sign my name in thick gray lines and the placement of my desk in all the classrooms, all were informed by this shadow.

My family around the dinner table was part of the shadow—the juicy meat in their mouths, the hot spurts of their arguments. I saw the chewed food slide to the corners of their mouths in mid-sentence. I'd seen Polina's strange oblong clothes, her severe chapeau, her dark eyebrows. I'd smelled the perfume in Polina's tall bottle, beheld its amber color, its austere elegance, the way the name of it was stretched in lean gold letters across the bottle. It was why I chose as my first friend Deirdre, who was blond, pale, with tidy thin lips, and who wore pleasant pastels. Was this what wicked was?

Leonard picked Joyce to read the third question. *"With the person unable to ask, you must begin yourself as it is written. You shall tell your child on that day saying, 'It is because of what the Lord did for me when I went free from Egypt.'"* Leonard knew that she was definitely not the person "unable to ask." She was all interrogation, all interruption.

*"The silent person just shows up."* My father smiled at me lovingly. *"Can it be that this child hears something different?"*

It sounded so familiar. It sounded like the inside of my dreams. No, it sounded like all the time. Seeing Cynthia, Corrie and Pat's mother, down the table, her graceful ringed fingers resting on the empty plate in front of her, I remembered, with a mild shock, one night when I was very young and had stayed overnight at Cynthia and Simon's house.

Cynthia had smelled to me of light sweetness, high and light-haired, glinting of jewelry, a voice waving, rolling serenely. I'd felt the ripples as they descended to my level flatten to undulations around me. Late that night, when Cynthia lay in a silky yellow gown on her bed, I had sleepwalked into their bedroom. I'd been striding in dream visions of butterflies, meadows, knowing only slightly that I was walking on a gray woolen rug cropped short and that there was no sun here, really, the light was off. Still, undeniably, there was a butterfly with large outstretched wings, just out of reach. It had led me into the room where they slept in their bed, long-legged, their marble bodies catching the moon. Suddenly, water cascaded, splashing in the grasses. Marshes. A bird leapt up from a huge tree, the butterfly faded in splendor. A light was flicked on. I stood there in wet pajamas, a dark pool beneath my feet. "What is this?"

"*True redemption,*" someone read, "*will come to the Jew only if he bears his name and every burden with gleaming courage and radiant nobleness.*"

Ernest and Alvin hovered at the French doors with bottles of wine poised for the next glass to be filled. They were early.

"The meal is served," Leonard announced, waving a regal arm at Alvin. Then I watched them enter, tall, Black, silent with trays of Elsie's food. They dipped and swayed around the table, making quiet talk with guests. They looked like tall plants; the seated people like bright flowers. I could not seem to trace my usual concern. In came the soup, ladled by Elsie in the kitchen, her face hot over the stove, lifting the pudgy matzo balls into the shallow china bowls. Hurrying and hurrying yet smooth in their black suits, Ernest and Alvin had arranged them onto trays. Then, gliding through the kitchen, the hall, into the empty living room where they stationed trays, so they could bring two soup bowls at a time out to the sunroom.

I took a few sips out of my large silver spoon. The soup was good and hot. The steam, rising into my nostrils, warmed me. What if I were standing at the head of a long medieval street, and people, astonished, pointed at me from upper story windows? What if I were standing at the head of the street, a stream of words screaming from my mouth, unstoppably? I understood then, at least for a moment, that I'd held something, a bird's egg, in my mouth, for years. *Crack it!* I thought. Become the sand crab, the purple starfish, and the underwater bracken swirling in the white sunlight.

I had probably already had three glasses of wine in my small cup. I felt the smooth large napkin draped over the folds of my dress, the antelope leaping, frozen, across it. My father was wreathed in smoke at his end of the table; my mother at the other end of the table, as if through a mist. Polina seemed unusually calm, with no judgment in her eyes. When I turned again to my Haggadah, I felt only permission, a sense of largesse, as if a practiced, warm hand had pushed me firmly out the door, then shut its chestnut brownness in afternoon light.

"Out of the depths," Leonard was reading, "I am called upon the Lord. He answered me with His deliverance. We shall not die but live."

All around me, the candlesticks, the yellow of the flowers, the smooth napkins, the world was adjusting, alive.

"We shall walk before the Lord in the Land of the Living." Each word, distinct, resounded. All, tangible, sound. Sound, a substance with a color all its own, sound, now whitish, rich like twilight on a country hill, violets.

"Passing through waters, amid signs and wonders, was this our people born."

The service, at its crescendo, ended. Everyone ambled, bumpingly, into the living room. I moved close to Joyce and found myself clumsily, utterly embraced. But I curled out of the slightly inebriated hug, the way it enfolded and seemed to obliterate me.

Tomorrow would be an ordinary day, though the refrigerator would be full of leftover lamb carefully wrapped in waxed paper and the apricot mousse would sag forlornly in glass containers. Leftover matzos would be scrunched back into boxes. I would be alone in my head all day.

**1967**

# *hoodwinked*

Perhaps I had imagined the whole scene, I thought for a minute; it seemed so unlikely. It seemed like a scene from Doris Lessing. But I couldn't think what a character from *The Golden Notebook* would do now. I thought, vaguely, that there might be some political issues the character would understand, but I couldn't see beyond the light in the salon, the dark in the hall. The whole world seemed very quiet and calm now that I was on my feet. So, at a loss for a reason not to, I returned to the salon. The door to the hall, open.

Jacov brushed proficiently, the bristle scraped my scalp. I sat primly, but my hair felt luxurious, falling heavy over my shoulders. Then I left to find my cabin room, my bed with the gray ship blanket. I wanted only to sit there and peer out the porthole at the half-sky, half-water, in leaping wavelets. Maybe I could settle into that horizon. The room would be empty since it was midday and my roommates would still be at lunch.

At the keyhole of the door, my hand was fluttering, the key rattling, as if the hole were oversized and the key like bones rattling. But when I reached for the doorknob, to steady myself, it opened easily. There, sprawled everywhere, were women.

In the center of the floor, with Tarot cards saturated in color, sat Mathilde, one of my cabin mates. Her hair was tied in a bright scarf. One of her eyes danced merrily, her other, fixed, gleaming, on the cards. Her smile was wide, stretched uncannily over her mouth, painted (did I imagine this?) beyond the mouth. Mathilde was just reaching for a card and held out a beseeching hand. Two women kneeled in front of Mathilde, twins, their pallid faces drained. "Ah," said Mathilde, in the red shimmery scarf, welcoming me with a limp arm.

"I've drawn the Eight of Swords for you. Here is a woman hoodwinked, her eyes bound shut. Swords surround her. Any messages that come are garbled. This isolation has a purpose, to avoid people you should not see, to miss events. You have been given time to mature. This card is about restriction but also about breaking free. See, she stands in a pool of water. If only she would look, she would see herself."

My heart raced. One of the twins grinned toothily and patted the wrist of the other in a tepid congratulatory way. The other stroked her own short hair over and over in unintended mockery of a caress. Mathilde waited for my response. She turned a few more cards and nodded, as the results seem to verify her first reading. "Does this mean anything to you?"

My arms, instructed by some new set of controls, reached out to the doorjamb. I stepped back behind myself, wishing I could lock the door and never come down this corridor again.

There was a hatbox in my parents' closet. It was a pentagonal box for one of Polina's fancy hats, with a Manhattan winter scene painted in black and yellow on its five panels. Couples skated on a barely rendered Rockefeller Center rink, the gentlemen in top hats, the ladies in small veils, their muffs in hand, their faces aquiline. The lid fit wonderfully. One lonely long-ago day, I had taken the box down and lifted the lid to let it fall a few times, snugly into place. Then I lifted the lid off the box. There was no hat inside but a lot of tissue paper, which I scrunched. Under the tissue, a shiny corner of a photograph showed. I felt a stack of pictures. In the dark and light top photo was my father, naked, his penis erect. I dropped the photo, only to see, in the next, my naked mother draped over a chaise, legs spread. I'd shoved the pictures under the white paper, horrified, heart pounding.

# *righteous indignation*

I rushed up to the deck to breathe. The air was warm, the sky overcast, people laughing. Here in the breezes on the deck, with the pleasant clink of glasses, waiters wandered among the passengers carrying drinks and pillows, magazines and suntan lotion. In their lounge chairs, Celia was dozing in glasses and a white bonnet, Bob reading. The world on deck seemed an orderly, predictable world. Surely there was an explanation for the weird behavior of the women in my room. It's always "a tall dark stranger." Just a coincidence that Jacov was dark, and not, now I thought of it, all that tall. The scene in the salon seemed, now, surreally calm. I hadn't been threatened, just detached, maybe even bemused. I tried out this interpretation, intrigued by my own sophistication. I hadn't gone hysterical; I'd hardly raised my voice, just that moment when the door seemed locked.

"Celia," I said suddenly, now able to speak, having summoned up a cosmopolitan perspective, "the strangest thing just happened." Celia turned her lipsticked mouth but did not remove the dark sunglasses.

"I was having my hair done." Did I imagine a sneer in Celia's thick lips? "I met him at the dance and found out he did hair, and so I went, you know, just to sort of not be a snob. And everything was as usual, but I must have been really tired. I fell asleep while my hair was drying, and then I woke up. And he, um, had put his tongue, um, sort of in me. And I left," I concluded rapidly.

Celia removed her glasses; Bob was staring too. I had somehow expected Celia to reassure me, to be a comforting nurse, but Celia was solemn. "You should report him. This should not have happened," she announced. My heart slowed, tiptoed. I remembered the night my family's poodle whelped. The dog, having produced one small apricot mound of puppy, stood shivering and guilty against the farthest wall of a newspaper-filled enclosure. The dog seemed to be expecting a beating.

"No," Celia was saying, even her lips pale, "what about the others, some other young single woman. Something must be done! If you need me to translate or anything, I will."

It was as if the breath had been knocked out of me and then, in a whoosh, I had breathed in new fresh air. No longer cowering in the face of Celia's cold analysis, it became clear to me: I was a free woman, like the women in *The Golden Notebook*. Swept up in the bracing vigor of righteousness. I would be a crusader for justice. "Thanks," I said, suddenly lighthearted, focused on a task for the good of others less sophisticated than I, who might, unlike me, be frightened by such an encounter.

Looking for the captain to report the incident, I was handed off, steward to steward, like Ginger Rogers, from one gold-braided handsome shoulder to the next. I glided the length of the ship, until I was whirled into an empty oval room with a rotunda roof and a closed circular walkway above. It was exhilarating having a purpose: find the captain. But now I stood, awkwardly, in a chairless room. When I looked up to a high walkway, sailors were looking down, pointing, their white teeth smiling, their dark heads close to one another. I expected to wait a few minutes, but I waited for over an hour. I sensed that my whole destiny as a grown woman depended upon my new moral indignation on behalf of others. I would not collapse. I determined that I would not even sit down on the floor.

At last I was summoned. Two officials escorted me into a windowless room where a number of men sat around a table. The captain was visible by difference. He was the smallest. He sat tidily, his arms covered in a frail froth of graying curls. The others were muscled and dark. Celia, who had promised to translate, was not present. My voice emerged quiet, quieter than I meant, and more shy. "Down there," was the best I could come up with, suddenly needing to appear virginal. The captain nodded while I spoke in English and heard it translated by one of the sailors. He turned side to side and made a comment in Hebrew. The sailors laughed in unison.

When I finished, he said, "Ah! Thank you. I am glad you have given this report, it will help so much." He spoke in fluent English, so why had my words been translated? "Yes," he continued, "I have wanted some evidence. I have a relative who would do well in his place."

I was confused. What web had ensnared me?

## *no time to run*

T here she is!" The blond woman, the social director, was striding down the corridor, wearing short shorts and cowboy boots, her once sleek hair stuck out all over her head in uncombed tufts. She looked like a hysterical Barbie doll. "You bitch!" she snarled. "How could you do that to him?" Her arms were raised, and she was heading toward me. I ran. The handles on the ship room doors merged to an elongated silver streak as I raced down corridors. The woman did not pursue, but I made a long circuit through the halls before I calmed down enough to enter one of the ship lounges where I hoped to find Devora maybe. As I entered, the small crowd turned silent and stared.

The glory I had imagined early in the trip had evaporated into an awful, shadowy realm. And there seemed no escape. A world of blame was the reward for pretending to be worldly, a woman. Finally, I slinked into my now empty room, shaky and numb.

Later, Devora, outside the door, called in, "I'm sure you haven't done anything so bad. Come on out." I liked the sound of Devora's voice, like some ointment soothed on chafed skin, creamy. But it was as if I didn't know language yet, only light and dark. "Can I bring you something from dinner?" Then, the footsteps away from the door and deep sleep.

The next morning I recovered enough to dress, to pack my small bag, for today was the day we were to dock in Israel. I sat alone on a bench on the ship while others milled around, chatting. I sat with my one small leather bag as the sun burned through the morning haze while we waited for docking permission. It grew warmer. Just as I rose to find some shade, Jacov approached. I had no time to run. He came close.

"I am sorry for what has happened," he said, quietly. I felt the heat of his arms. I couldn't speak. I didn't know which part he was sorry for. "Would you come to meet my lawyer and finish it all up?" Jacov asked, handing me a small paper with an address. My tongue moved thickly, unable to form words. I said nothing.

In the slow customs line, I watched my small bag, dully. There was really nothing in it but my white wool dress, a shawl, and the black-and-white skirt. I heard my name called over and over again before I recognized it. It was in American English.

**1967**

# *hashish?*

O ver here." Ben, my friend from New York, was calling. I had forgotten I'd written that I was coming to Israel. That I'd asked if he would still be there. That I had any other life.

Ben took me to a café where we ate falafel. He listened patiently, his eyebrows furrowed, as I told him most of what had happened, emphasizing the surreality. At the end, he took my hands and pressed a moist-petaled kiss on them. Then he took the small square of paper and read the address. He knew where in Haifa the meeting would be. As I licked the spicy cooked crumbs and drank the fresh coffee, I began to breathe, even to smile at Ben. Here we were, after all, in Israel. Here was Ben.

On the afternoon that we arrived at the lawyer's office, I'd decided to go in alone. "I'll pick you up across the street in an hour," Ben said quietly at the door. "If you are not out by then, I'll be up to rescue you." He was kind but serious.

There were yellow curtains in the window and magazines in the waiting room of the lawyer's office. The only other person was a woman with white-blond hair and Carnaby Street clothes, a slick, very mini pink-striped skirt. Her legs were long and creamy. "Pretty, *yafeh*," I said, indicating the woman's skirt. The woman tossed her shiny hair and smiled, as if we were equals. Then the woman touched the hem of my skirt and said clearly in English, "This too is very fine. I like this."

Her nut-brown eyes stared right into my avoiding green ones. "Don't do this to him. Don't do it. We are to be married in a month." She was leaning in toward me and grasped one of my wrists, awkwardly. Her hands were cool and soft. "I know he does things, but he is a good man. The captain is trying to frame him," she warned urgently. "Just please . . ." she said, and left, the words trailing.

Should I ally with the pretty woman who seemed sincere, who forgave Jacov's flirtations? Was that what it was? In the light of day, the yellow curtains, maybe it was just my own naiveté and Celia's righteous response that confused me?

The door to the office opened. Two men sat on one side of a wooden table. There was a single chair on the other side, for me. The room gave off a wooden male smell. The men had jowly faces.

"So," said the first, with a leonine head of tawny hair and eyebrows. He had a knowing legalistic scowl that reminded me of my father. The other man had gray hair slicked to his head, coating it like a seal's. His nose pointed aggressively. His very skin seemed to sniff, to be searching for some bad odor. He himself, down to the fingernails that tapped on the table, was scrupulously clean. Was I the source of his down-turned lips? He was annoyed, slightly disgusted. "So," the lion repeated. There was a long moment during which I sat opposite the two men, aware that they were waiting but not sure for what. I was much more frightened here than in the beauty salon. These men, with hair growing on their large fingers, waited in silence. The man with the tawny hair reached around and scratched his shoulder.

"Will you make it simple, sign this paper, and admit here that you did ask Jacov to sell you the hashish?" I stared at him. His huge eyes were thunderous.

"Hashish?" I repeated. I had heard the word but never said it. It had a nice sound to it, like a lullaby, a whisper to a child, *hashish*. But I didn't even know what it looked like, only the sound, which I said again, "Hashish?" Both lawyers lighted cigarettes and waited. Dumbfounded, I watched the smoke curl from both cigarette tips in dizzy spirals. Nothing I could hold on to stayed still. I shut my eyes and took my spinning head in both hands.

"We will give you a few minutes to think it over." The two lawyers left the room. My head slumped to the table, which seemed to be revolving slowly around in one direction, my feet on the floor in another. It was as if I were Alice in Wonderland, but I didn't know who stole which tart from whom. Tweedledee and Tweedledum were twiddling pens and it had all become my fault, and I was sinking. I actually dozed for a few minutes. In my little sleep, allegiances had formed. I was for the Knave and his Lady and against the selfish King. I would sign the sheet; I would make a little order. I'd sign the silly paper, my signature without meaning meant nothing, I decided, existentially.

Writing my name slowly, I realized that I hadn't written any words at all, for weeks. It looked like my signature at nine. I remembered a story my father had told me about a time when he was young. He'd been playing baseball on a Saturday, which he was not supposed to do in his observant family. He was hungry on the way home and he bought a hot dog. The trouble was that it was a nonkosher hot dog. He told the story with a wink. What I'd always understood was that it was okay. That God didn't really mind him playing and certainly didn't begrudge him the hot dog, since he was a hungry boy. The universe had more latitude than the rules would indicate.

The lawyers returned, the slim one following the thick. Both thanked me, shook my hand and showed me out, early for Ben, into the empty street. A warm breeze swayed grape leaves side to side over my head where I stood in the crook of a doorway. I gazed at my own tan leather sandals; the ground was a comfort.

# talcum powder

B en took me back to his Aunt Ida and Uncle Morris's house
in Tel Aviv. I was welcomed in Yiddish, hugged, and
accepted as if long awaited. Ben and Morris had stripped to
their undershirts and sat on the apartment balcony to catch
any little bit of evening air that might arrive. They spoke
Hebrew rapidly. I couldn't understand the words, only Ida's
embrace. Ida touched my hair to tell me how pretty it was.
Ida, though she probably looked different, reminded me of
my great-grandmother who I'd only heard about, Polina's
grandmother, the only person Polina described without bit-
terness. My great-grandmother had baked, had sung, and
had loved flowers.

In the corner of the kitchen, Ida and I ate fresh bread
and jam. Ida's eyes twinkled as she gathered a load of sheets.
Her arms were short; their upper slopes swayed extrava-
gantly. I offered her my younger arms but could barely carry
half the loads Ida hoisted. Ida slid the sheets through her

uplifted arms, wrung them. I held my sheet in small portions steadily over my bucket and twisted. The yield was only a minor trickle of soapy water. Later, Ida guided me down narrow wooden steps to a cool basement, a closet-sized room where the dry sheets were piled on a basket. Ida lifted a fitted sheet in her two nimble plump arms. Expertly, she lined the hemmed rims into a straight ridge and tucked one corner cleanly into the other. In a deft swish, all four corners were cradled in the one looped corner. Then they were stroked, creased into a flat, almost ironed, square. Back home, if sheets were to be folded, they were grasped by two sets of unwilling hands, Joyce's and mine. The process quickly became political: Which would force the other to come to her side? I didn't register that this was the first time I'd thought of my sister and mother since the incident on the boat. Both were dispelled by the scent of Ida's talcum powder drifting around the room.

# the Black Russian

When the summer ended, I was scheduled to return to the US. My layover in Paris was three hours, and I had the equivalent of ten dollars. Alone in Orly airport, I suddenly recaptured the sense of poise I'd begun to feel at the start of the trip to Israel. I strolled into the airport bar and ordered a Black Russian. I'd read about bars, and about Black Russians. I took a high stool at the bar, and no one contested my claim.

The drink arrived in a crystal glass with a small beard of white froth around the edges. How easy it was to play the role. One sip of sweetness circled my mouth. I felt the alcohol cleaning and tranquilizing me. For the three hours, I sipped. Each inhalation a vaporous whisper, each exhalation a breathful of alcohol. Here, anonymous at the bar, serenity settled on me. The very bones in my hands gracefully displayed my fingers on the fine wood.

I slept the whole flight home.

Leonard was at the airport to meet me. From a distance, he looked short, stood crookedly, one hip higher than the other. In the world, he would not have caught my eye. But when he lifted his hand to wave, I remembered the warmth of that raised palm and the former enormity of it. Now he was gruff.

"Where are your bags? Your plane was late, you know." I had no response when he asked, "How was your trip?" since he seemed to be asking about the flight itself, the least important detail of my ten months out of the country.

I suggested that we stop on the way home. I was trying to slow the reentry process down. Leonard took me to Duke Z's restaurant. Duke's served massive meat sandwiches to Washington's lawyers and politicians. The tables were large, to accommodate the physiques of his clientele, and far apart to allow for deals. I felt trim and traveled and ordered salad. My father ordered hot pastrami with Dijon mustard. He held the meat tenderly between slices of dark bread.

"I want to tell you something that happened," I said, before I'd thought about it. His dark eyes were a shining contrast to the beige mustard in his sandwich. This telling was different from the time I'd told Ben. I wanted my father to see how accomplished I'd become, how cosmopolitan. But I was emphasizing at all the wrong points. I worried I was going on in too much detail about the salon appointment itself to avoid the next scene. "Suddenly, his tongue was in me," I plunged on, hoping my father wouldn't ask for more details. His brow was so tightly clenched that I couldn't see the skin in the crevice. He puffed on his after-meal cigar. Relieved to be past the sexual scene and on to the ethical, I was comforted that we would share a certain cynicism. He would appreciate my wit, my sleight of hand, my ducking under the false gate so deftly by signing the silly piece of paper.

"Did he try to contact you again?" Leonard suddenly demanded, leaning forward on the table as if he might push off from it into a whirlwind of orders.

"No," I answered, quietly. I'd forgotten that my father believed in the sanctity of the legal document, not in the exigencies of travel. For him, there was no foreign moment. A waiter arrived with cake and ice cream we hadn't ordered, from Duke, who tipped his head in tribute.

Moving his head side to side as if to rid himself of some substance clinging to his face, he began. "Listen very carefully. I am only going to say this once. You have been extremely lucky. But I don't want repercussions. Does he have our home address?"

I shook my head, sad that the event had been miscon-strued and I'd never be able to reclaim it. "If he ever does try to reach you, you are to let me know immediately." I laughed at the autocratic command, catching sight of my clean sun-bleached nails, remembering the scent of myself in the sun.

"This is very serious," Leonard interrupted.

I nodded. I noticed I was clutching the napkin in my lap. I wondered what danger Leonard anticipated. A familiar bleak misery filled me. I nodded because his eyes were beady bright. I agreed, because I understood that all he cared about was my name, my name written in my hand, the only part of the incident I'd actually decided to do.

"You are not to talk to anybody about this, not to anyone. Ever." Leonard clamped the damp cigar between his lips. He drew air through it until the cigar began to glow at the tip. My whole self seemed to thicken. My arms became heavy. I reverted to the time, years before, when Joyce and I were awakened, groggy, early in the morning and dressed in identical dresses of gauzy printed roses and taken to the airport. It was to have been a surprise, the trip to Los Angeles. But I was only dazed, heavy, with no will and no wish, my eyes lidded in submission to the weight of my parents' decisions.

When we rose to leave the restaurant table, I felt my skirt's embrace, the definition of myself, from the small firm waistband down the rocky boulders of my hips, straight down. I stood, secretly rejuvenated. Leonard was still clumsily peeling dollars onto the table, his cigar dangling in his mouth. I realized then that I, in my own body, was separate from him. I would navigate my own course. Standing, I felt strength in my muscles, the code in my very skeleton that meant I would walk into the complicated world, myself, alone and sufficient.

# PART TWO

# 1968

# *eyes like blue crystal*

The first time I walked with Tom, my senior year, his galoshes stamped a dirty autumn puddle as high as my swinging-clear hair. When I leaned back to see the halo of sky, he named the constellations. He kicked water up again to my eyes so that the stars spread as diffused broken lights. I'd returned from Israel to Kenyon, which seemed small to my newly enlarged eyes. Tom, though, was tall, confident, the best of America. His gaze level, his stance uncompromising. He was the opposite of Ben, who was diminutive and displaced.

Tom looked up at the sky. "Wait," he said, "the moon is not supposed to be there tonight!" Then he figured out why the aberration had occurred. His explanation made sense to him, so he accepted the moon's location. That he would question the moon and rely more on his own calculation, that he had such confidence in his own powers of deduction, was enviable. I laughed and laughed at the relief of it. His eyes were bright blue, and they turned right on me and held me. I felt that he had stared straight into the future, a blue highway straight across the country.

Tom was a dorm counselor. His self-contained height and official leadership added to his appeal. He reminded me of high school football players. (I didn't know enough about football to notice that his shoulders were much too narrow and undeveloped to play. I didn't notice that he lacked the camaraderie that would have come from playing on a team.) What I did notice was the all-American clean-cut stature of him. He was the new world, the Anglo-Saxon American. He looked out over my head and seemed to see great distances. He had plans. He had a data entry job in the brand-new university computer lab. He was part of the real world. And he looked at me, with sharply focused intent.

Tom had first noticed me in the dorm lounge, where men and women were draped in the chairs, denouncing the Vietnam War. Tom had sat in a corner, apparently, and watched me climb purposefully up and down the stairs. The loungers seemed adolescent to me, or so I'd convinced myself. I had the secret of experience, of having survived the experience on the boat, of being worldly.

———

In all the pictures I ever saw of him as a child, Tom's eyes, round blue stones, pierced his mother, Blanche. In one, Tom had just tied his own shoes with chubby white laces, tamed them until they lay flat and butterflied across his foot. He looked up in the picture, proud of his accomplishment. Even as an adult, Tom tied his shoes methodically and with pride.

I remembered my own pride as I trotted across the kitchen floor when I was six. My mother had told me to start the oven. I'd heaved open the oven door and felt the tug back of it. About to pull down the door, and expose the red veined and black interior, I'd been frightened and brave. I turned the round dial that read ON/OFF, smoothly, all the way up to the top of the dial. I heard the pleasant hiss of gas, then went into the dining room to set the table. This I had accomplished with great concentration, laying the knives straight, their serrated edges civilly away from the plates, the forks in forthright perpendicularity to the table edge. I'd folded the paper napkins, creasing them as straight as I could. Suddenly, I heard Polina in the kitchen scream "Jesus Christ!" Polina howled, hands on the sides of her face singed by the gas explosion, her black hair sizzled gray.

I didn't mention the memory to Tom.

If he had peeked into his drawer on school mornings, I imagined Tom would have found stacks of white T-shirts, button-down shirts, their folds even, their fronts ironed, flat and clean, ironed blue jeans and five sets of white socks. He would have been allowed to take one from each pile. His mother chose clothes for him that all matched, no matter which he pulled from each stack. The pants were bought big, hemmed until he grew, then the hem was let out. When they passed to his brother, they were hemmed up again. A whole different interaction with clothes than at my house.

In summer birthday pictures, he showed up in nice blue shorts and jackets his mother sewed for him. There were pictures of her in full skirts and tight curls. Summers, Tom dived into some waterhole with his dad, sharpened his penknife, chose turquoise blue-and-white gimp cord to make a key ring. I knew that Tom's key ring would look just like the picture in the crafts book. His mother or father would have taught him exactly how to do it. It made me remember one summer when I was seven, in the public pool near our house.

Before our own pool was installed, we went to the public pool off Connecticut Avenue. Seeking quiet and moving away from some boys jumping noisily in elasticized shorts and some older girls with wet ponytails who were splashing the surface, shrieking, I'd swum underwater, deeper and deeper into the turquoise quiet. I frog-kicked my legs in gigantic fearless thrusting. Suddenly, I was stopped. A young man, who thought he was saving me, caught me in his long arms, which he clenched around my middle. I was trapped, netted, and lifted from the water, sputtering. The air was so shapeless after the even and oddly familiar pressure of the water, so bright, and so broken that I burst into tears. My young savior delivered me, sobbing hiccups, to my mother.

As I spent more time with Tom, I imagined that he had grown up surrounded by uncles named Earl, Claude, Max, Eugene, and Willis; tall men with suspenders who drank coffee and ate pies. Their wives Lucy, Clara, Mildred, Vivian, and Rhoda would have worn heels and stockings, made cheese sandwiches, and wrapped them for picnics in waxed paper, the ends folded into overlapping triangles.

At night, on Tom's bedroom walls, yellow-scarfed cowboys probably crooned and high-booted rangers lassoed cattle. In the morning, there would be toast and jam, his father at the paper, his mother at the sink. Not like my mornings, when Joyce and I sat side by side at the kitchen table where Elsie silently served us breakfast and left us to it, to get on with polishing the candlesticks, the Brasso smell filling the whole of the kitchen. Polina would be long gone to the hospital and Leonard out of town.

The more of Tom's orderly life I imagined, the more of my own isolation I remembered. Once I'd found a hole half way up the dirt wall beneath our porch. Peering in, I saw a whole room only two feet high with a dirt floor under the porch. I crawled onto the rumpled dirt, then back to the most dark and most distant corner. My face was close to earth, my nose full of its dryness. One low window let in light, and I moved around on my stomach, legs behind me, until I faced the opening. I stared at the dry crumpled peaks and, somehow, fell asleep, buoyed by the hard clods.

When I woke, a horror rose in me. I shimmied forward on my belly, my hands and feet clawing at the dry dirt, pulling me forward so fast, so straight that my upper body was halfway out over the exit hole before I had to stop, retreat, turn over, and rotate to send my legs out first to touch the ground. My heart pounded. My spine arched as my feet felt for the ground. My chest and head slithered through as if I were dancing the limbo, out the brick-and-dirt opening. Landed, I ran outside to breathe. I'd probably been hidden beneath the porch for a late afternoon hour, and no one had noticed. Polina and Leonard would have been at work. Elsie, inside, was probably listening to a soap opera, ironing, and Joyce away at a friend's house.

———

By the time his mother waved Tom off to college, his shoulders glamorous, his height impressive, his eyes sharply focused on the future, Blanche might only have come close enough to smell the aftershave. When I actually met her, I was struck by how much Tom's mother seemed to admire her son. I didn't know how to understand a mother who made room for her child's maturity. Was it Blanche's timidity? That's what Polina would have thought, timidity and subservience—Blanche was such a tidy little creature in her apron and little heels. I imagined that she had shed tears, and told Tom to write.

Polina told me once that she'd decided, when she was in Scotland talking to some woman about how they would treat the children they would have, that the most important thing was to keep your own life first. The children should stay in their place. I was certain that Blanche and her husband had designed their life around their miraculous boys.

The next time Blanche had seen Tom, at Thanksgiving, the Vietnam War was in full swing and Tom was changed. Blanche would have observed the way his hair had crept out of its tidy frame around his ears and lay in an oily blond lank against his back. All the matched madras cotton college shirts she'd bought and packed had disappeared. All that was left were limp T-shirts with unintelligible typography and logos. Blanche would have said nothing. She probably bit her lips hard till the teeth cut a sharp edge to keep quiet.

I had no close friends. No one knew that I sneaked over to Tom's room at night. No one knew that Tom's body was pearly white. His eyes, like blue crystal, held me in all their facets. Tom kept me in his line of vision while he caressed me. His stare continued, urgent. No one knew. No one needed to know the discomfort of waking up before dawn, before the men in his dorm might wake, when I slipped down the back stairs with my tights clutched in my hands, not willing to take the time to pull them up; not, more to the point, not willing to encounter the dampness between my legs I had not been able to dry. I hardly considered the indignity of having Tom check the late-night path to the men's bathroom so I could dart in and out, heart pounding. I had decided it was an adventure, risqué, and my due.

*seen*

The story of our parents' meeting had been told to us repeatedly. When Leonard first saw Polina, he was the head of a boy's camp and she was considering being the doctor at the corresponding girl's camp. Joyce absorbed the story for its love-at-first-sight authenticity. I saw it in little dabs of color.

Polina, recently returned from her Nevada residency for divorce, went, reluctantly, to the first meeting for counselors at an upstate New York camp, "at the Knickerbocker Hotel, in Manhattan." (The Knickerbocker part was easy to remember and amusing, since it was told with such certainty of recognition. Though I hardly knew any of New York, and certainly not this hotel, I could have chimed in to say it. In fact, I sometimes did mouth this part under my breath.) It hadn't been Polina's idea to work at a camp. It was her mother who thought Polina needed a break, a summer by a lake. Polina was probably haughty, probably felt superior to these Americans who didn't have medical degrees, who hadn't been to Europe, and who certainly hadn't been married and divorced already. She arrived at the pre-camp meeting in a white suit, which, I knew, would have shown off her newly bronzed skin. Polina would certainly have been tan. No doubt, she took her Bain de Soleil to Nevada and lay at the hotel pool with a book, smoking and casually checking that her skin was darkening by the hour. She'd probably had a two-piece bathing suit, strapless on top. That's what she wore at the pool off Connecticut Avenue.

Actually, it was a little confusing, since Polina always mentioned the white suit she wore to the Knickerbocker, and Leonard always referred to some bright red sweater she must have worn to the first camp counselor party. They both agreed that they noticed each other. Even objectively, Leonard was a handsome man. He had thick curly hair and a rolling set of eyebrows that could be ferocious or deeply comic, like a Shakespearean commedia masque. Polina, telling the story, said that Leonard seemed to beam at all the ladies. She "thought he was a flirt."

When Polina arrived at the camp, she was picked up by someone else, not by Leonard, and she was clearly peeved. The fellow who'd picked her up at the station spent the whole drive back to the camp telling her how great Leonard was. She didn't realize that it was "a ploy." It was never clear to me what parts of the story had been shaped by retrospect. But I was secretly pleased by the notion that Leonard got the best of her. For those few moments of the story, it's as if he could see through her. But soon Leonard always said, "She showed up in a magnificent red sweater," and Polina usually said, "There's no need to go on, Len." I imagined the red of the sweater, tomato red. The sweater, as if it were the paper clothes of a cutout cardboard doll with little tabs to attach it, was the focal point. I couldn't even really imagine Polina in her red sweater. Was she like one of those pinup girls in the Coca-Cola ads in gas stations? Much later in my life, when my husband-to-be first noticed me coming down the stairs of a dormitory, I was thrown back to the question of what had been seen by my father.

# *inadequate*

They all came, Joyce, Leonard, and Polina, on the very humid day of my graduation. The air was crowded with moisture. My head was crowded. Leonard and Polina stayed in the Campus Inn and complained about it. The room was "inadequate," Polina announced, oblivious to the volume of her loud voice in the shared mumble of the Midwest.

"I want the coffee *after* breakfast, not *with*," Polina told the student who was our waitress at breakfast and who was rushing to fill the orders of a whole room of visiting parents, most of whom had dreamy proud looks on their wide flat faces.

"Joyce, stop squirming." Joyce wasn't exactly squirming, but she was uncomfortable and mystified. She and I were supposed to share a room the night before, but I hadn't been there and told her not to tell.

The sky was as warm and constricting as the southern sky of Maryland, so it felt like home and I was catapulted back.

When Tom joined us at the end of breakfast at the Campus Inn, I was briefly relieved by his clean, clear height. My parents had to look up to him. Though he wouldn't graduate until the next year, he told them he'd got a high-paying job for the summer, in Maryland. Joyce was impressed that I had a boyfriend with a job.

## tell me what to do

That fall, Tom returned to school for his last year. I went to New York to work for the Ted Bates Advertising Agency. I'd gotten a liberal arts degree in English with a few education courses, and I was working while I decided where to teach. My whole New York apartment was one room. I leaned out the fifth-story window and twisted to catch a glimpse of the Hudson River. I wrote home, on my own at last, that I had an apartment with a river view. For a while, it felt as if I were living.

I'd taken a single set of cutlery with me, a set Leonard had bought me years before, antique, from Portobello Road. It was a gold-colored metal and smaller than the ordinary. No matter what the meal, I sliced it with my small gold knife and ate it with my tiny four-pronged fork. In the mornings, I stared at a postcard of an 1800s ice skater in a fitted dress and red peplum jacket. The woman had a brown muff and a red hat on her dark hair. She was a figure on ice, with a large sun looming over half the sky, an early advertisement for the *Morning Sun*.

One time, I awoke in the middle of the night, shivering. I wasn't cold, my legs were warm in the sofa bed, but I was terrified. I couldn't move except my arms. With great difficulty, I pulled a phone over and called Tom, at school in Ohio. In a sleepy responsible voice, he suggested that I call the emergency room, that even though I wasn't dying of a gun wound, it was an emergency.

"Get down here to the ER immediately!" they advised. I lay in bed, tears streaming down both sides of my face, trying to plan how to get to the ER from the fifth floor if I couldn't move. I'd thought that they'd send an ambulance. But they never mentioned that option. What did that mean? Was it naive to expect such service?—the kind of thing a well-off suburban girl would expect—that just didn't happen in the real world? My eyes whirled the square four walls. I understood for a moment how alone I was. Finally, since I couldn't figure out what else to do, I lowered myself off the bed by stacking pillows to soften the descent. I dragged myself to the door and, sitting on one step at a time, bumped down to the first floor. With each thump, some mobility returned. So apparently, the hospital had been right to know that I was not really immobile. How did they know?

From my perch on the outside step, I hailed a cab. The driver was a middle-aged man with an open face, who laughed with me at my story. He drove me through the finally quiet streets. "I should do this for fun. See Manhattan at 4 a.m. in my pajamas," I said.

The emergency room doctors decided that I just needed some Valium, some muscle relaxant. When I awoke the next day, all was well. I'd wanted Tom to take care of me, tell me what to do. But I also wanted the delightful discovery that disaster could melt into magic. That I could be safe and sound in a cab riding through the city in the middle of the night with a kind driver, who would drive me to the hospital and home again before the sun rose. I just couldn't trust that magic enough to let go of Tom's firm hand.

One night while I was still in college, I'd been working on a paper about Matisse's *Red Studio* for an art appreciation class. Outside there was a torrential thunderstorm heaving against the windows. The more I stared at the *Red Studio* and tried to articulate my sense of it, with its deep, deep-red walls and the bits of vine drifting at all levels, detached from the walls but somehow related, the more I saw there were no boundaries in the painted room. That the red went much deeper than the wall, deep into crashing sound. The wall was pretend, an artifice. The red was real. This idea terrified me. I shrank from it. I thought of Tom, who would stand by the integrity of the artificial wall. I chose what I thought was sanity. But in the paper I wrote, the reds were glorified. On the page, I could almost see the truth in what I wrote.

# *hypnotized*

Tom planned to pick me up from New York for a cross-country trip over his December break, to see New Mexico where he'd grown up. I decided to bake fruitcakes as hostess presents with a hint of Christmas in them, proofs of my suitability in the culture I imagined I'd encounter. I probably couldn't have accounted for the Betty Crocker image I had of a woman who would bake. One Saturday, I went to the Lower East Side to poke around dried fruit barrels for nuts and dried cherries, apricots and fresh pears. I followed a recipe, drenching the succulent pears in deep bowls of brandy in the one-room apartment. For three weeks the twelve little cakes hovered and aged in drawers, on top of the refrigerator, on the windowsill, several under the sofa bed, one on top of the small TV. Even after I wrapped each one in aluminum foil, they continued to reek and hypnotize.

In December, Tom arrived in his secondhand green Chevrolet for the cross-country trip. We would meet Tom's relatives, people I'd only seen in *Life* magazine, women with permed thin ash-blond hair, in aprons, split-level homes with pictures of sons in football uniforms and daughters at proms. We ate tuna casseroles and played after-dinner games. At night I washed delicately and dried with the pale guest towels, and tried, desperately, not to soil them. Of course we were given separate rooms; it was the sixties.

Tom and I consumed many of the fruitcakes ourselves, cramming crumbly and heavily alcoholed chunks into our mouths at rest stops when he decided not to spend money on food.

One time, I was at the wheel in New Mexico; Tom slept, smiling. No one else was driving the midnight road. I pulled over to stretch my legs. Stars throbbed in the sky, closer than I'd ever seen. I was thrilled. I didn't wake him.

## why wait?

The next summer, after Tom graduated, seated across from me in a red restaurant, he did an analysis. "I can't see any good reason not to get married," he stated, as if a little surprised. I hadn't known he was looking for reasons not to.

"Yes, OK, fine," I said, bemused. Getting married seemed distant and unreal. What was real was that we were eating chicken, dining with white napkins, out to lunch on a Saturday. It was the first time we had eaten in such a restaurant.

Back at home, Leonard sat with his wide tan legs opened, leveraged so he could sit upright on his haunches in spite of his heft, his naked brown belly bulging, as Tom and I came up the path to the house that day. All summer, Leonard had seen me draped, a vine of arms, around this blond gentile. Leonard had noted the lips of the boy, two slim parallel lines, noted the pens poking out of his white shirt pocket. My father could barely look at me, his own child, could hardly stand to see my green eyes doting on those blue ones. Leonard could not prevent me, but he could take over. He turned to Tom and me, a slight grimace beneath his grin.

"How about getting married next week in that case, why wait?" said Leonard. He leaned back in his deck chair by the pool, his belly so shiny he almost reflected the flickering shadows of airplanes as they flew toward National Airport.

Joyce was in Europe for the summer, and Polina and Leonard were scheduled to travel that fall. When Leonard suggested that we marry in just a few days, I did ask, "But what about Joyce?" How did we all convince ourselves to subordinate the wedding to those other plans?

Leonard and Polina's own wedding was an event that only the two of them attended. The excuse then was war-time; the reason was also that they didn't know how to cir-cumvent each of their families' insistence on an orthodox Jewish wedding. Neither Polina nor Leonard was interested. Maybe they'd always felt that weddings were a waste of time, of money, and not the point anyway. Once the deed was done, the families accepted the marriage.

I understood that there would be no party, and I was relieved but also interrupted. I had not even begun to imag-ine myself as going-to-be-married. I hadn't yet thought of discussing the possibility with my father. But as if prescient, Leonard asked Tom that very day, half jokingly, what his intentions were. And Tom, who dealt with comments lit-erally and seriously, answered, "Actually, my intention is to marry your daughter." So here we were, speeding down a corridor.

# extractions

The information I'd gleaned about my mother's divorce was sparse after the doctor from Canada. I knew what I was missing . . . probably some reference to sex. Of course, I'd never ask. Instead, I imagined her return to her husband in Edinburgh wearing a blue traveling suit and a small white hat with a blue trim. Her dark eyes would appear black, her skin dark, in all ways a contrast to William, who, I now imagined, had pale freckled skin, like the underside of a trout.

She'd only mentioned two repercussions of her ill-fated marriage. She told me about William's mother visiting hers to speak for Bill. And she talked about earning money for her divorce. William's mother, all gussied up, had marched up to Polina's mother's general store in Paterson, New Jersey—not to order ribbons or fabric or flour. She was there to speak to the mother of the girl who had ruined her boy, "taken the best year of his life. Make her take him back." My grandmother, apparently, dismissed the mother-in-law: "Polina makes up her own mind."

Was there any other situation in her life when her mother spoke up on Polina's behalf?

Polina described her next phase matter-of-factly. She claimed that she didn't hold a grudge. The fault was in "marrying the wrong man." In those days, one had to go to Nevada, where incompatibility qualified one for divorce. "You had to live there for six weeks to be a resident," she explained offhandedly. She'd "got a job in New York" in the Women's House of Detention to earn money for her divorce, which was to be a no-fault.

Polina was the staff physician. The women were brought to her. She examined them—their eyes, their skin—to see "if they had been beaten up," to see if they were pregnant or not, and to see if they had concealed weapons. Only once, she said, she found a small abalone-shell-covered pocket-knife in an inmate's vagina. She had extracted it.

The notion of "finding" something in a vagina was an eye-opener. What an odd place to look. Then the word, "extract," startled me.

When Polina had earned enough to not work for six weeks, she moved to Nevada to establish residency. She has told me that she went horseback riding to "kill the time."

Polina had taken me to horseback riding lessons when I was six. She had nice leather boots from England, with lit-tle straps around the ankle. She wore jodhpurs and had rid-ing gloves. But I, even at six, could tell that she was nervous around horses. The plan was that Polina would have a private lesson and so would I. It was the first in a series of classes Polina took while we daughters were growing up. There were so many pastimes of the rich that she hankered for. She took tennis lessons, went skiing (starting at fifty), took ice-skating lessons, and joined an ice-skating club.

At my first riding lesson, I was put on a large palomino mare with broad, flat withers. The teacher, wisely, told me just to lie down. So I spent a blissful hour lying on the patient broad back of a horse, watching creamy clouds roll across the Maryland spring sky. It was a perfect introduction. The faint whiff of horse drifted up, the regular clomp of horse hooves heavy on the dry dirt.

Riding lessons were the only lessons that I actually enjoyed. By the time I heard about my mother riding out in Nevada, I had a pretty good idea of what that must have meant. I imagined her all decked out in the right clothes, with her knees flapping uselessly on the sides of the creature. Her leather-gloved hands would hold the reins slack, until she'd have to turn the beast. Then she'd pull her hand way out to turn the horse's head. If the horse was tired, as it probably was, if it was for hire near some hotel in Nevada, it probably just stood there with its neck rubbered around to the right or left. Then Polina would kick it. I could just see her whacking at the horse with her boots, saying, "Go!" in an unconvincing, commanding tone.

# blue

I was let out of Polina's car with one hour to choose a dish
pattern. The store had no other customers, only plates and
silverware. I stared a long time at a white plate with a slim
cranberry strip. It made me sad. Then, I saw a sugar bowl
with a zany little lemon for a handle. Bluebird, the pattern
was called, though the bird, only a small element of the
design, was an exotic yellow parrot. The pattern was full of
random citrus fruits, amusing. So I picked it, thinking I had
thus asserted myself by my antagonism to convention. I'd
never considered what dishes I would want when I married.
In fact, I'd never considered that I would marry.

During the week, Tom's parents, Blanche and Al, hosted
an engagement party. It was a small gathering, only us, the
suddenly affianced, and our parents. Blanche made cherries jubilee. The cherries were the "new" color, dusty rose.
Blanche was trying hard to be correct. The napkins matched
the cherries. Polina stood with Blanche and looked at Tom

across the room slurping the cherries. "They are his favorites," Blanche confided.

"I hope he cuts his goddamn hair before the wedding," said Polina.

For the wedding, I wore a light blue, thick-skinned dress, Polina a mint green, Blanche a pink. Polina had taken me to Garfinckel's Department Store for Fine Apparel and sat in the dressing room with me, smoking Chesterfields. "No, don't show us white dresses," she'd snapped at the saleswoman. "You'd never be able to wear it for anything else," she told me. But I knew that white was supposed to be for virgins. At least this time, Polina did not mention that my hips were too big. She just sat smoking, fuming. Was she impatient at the inappropriate suggestions? Or that there was such a small inventory? How many people got married in a week, in August, and didn't want white? I thought the task we'd set must be a little daunting to the saleswoman. Or was Polina just angry at me for marrying Tom? Not that there was anyone else to choose from.

The dress we picked was a compromise. Polina liked it because it was a powder blue. She was the one who suggested that they shorten it to the "mini" length. She also picked out some silver platform shoes. It was 1969, and Polina was always aware of fashion. I liked it because it had fake jewels in two rows down the front and reminded me of Julie Christie in *Doctor Zhivago*, jeweled against the cold. Never mind that I was about to be married in Washington, DC, in August and a scorcher was predicted.

No one in the wedding party ever wore her dress again. The civil servant sported a crew cut. The ceremony was the most minimal reading of the law by the crew cut who swatted at a few mosquitoes in the course of it. The traffic on Cherry Lane was audible throughout the ceremony. We kissed at the appointed moment, and Leonard, in the background, murmured, "Not now, later." He got a laugh. Every time we found each other's eyes, Leonard barked, "Not now, later."

"Later" was the hotel room that Leonard had booked halfway downtown. The champagne from dinner draped my brain with a milky film. My eyes shut tight, and so did Tom's. Overfed, we slept, dazed, too hot, under the saffron-colored blanket in August, in Washington, DC. Now that it was "later," we could only sleep in separate thick dreams.

# safe by association

Tom's first job was at an actuarial firm in DC. After we were married, I began shopping at Sears. The clothes were as light as spring pancakes, racks and racks of light thin blouses, four for ten dollars, pastel prints. It was amazing how much could be acquired for how little money. I proceeded, dutiful and wifely, thinking this must be economizing.

Tom had decided to buy bicycles, ten-speed bicycles, a year ahead of the craze that swept America. He bought us each a bicycle with the money he made. Mine was a neat white Peugeot, a small fine thoroughbred, and Tom's larger, a blue Schwinn. We set out on a newly paved Rock Creek Park road, dark black asphalt against the early spring green. *He's always aware of coming crazes*, I thought. I'd be safe now, safe by association. Oddly, I, who used to pedal, ponytailed and agile, to visit my friend Deirdre was reduced, suddenly, to awkward anxiety—as if I'd never mounted a bicycle before. I heard myself asking my shiny new husband how to do whatever it was that needed doing. The high-pitched whining of the new brakes distracted me from any hint of abandon. "They just need to be broken in," Tom assured me.

All that summer Tom tore down city streets that were not accustomed to cyclists. At rush hour he rode to work, then he returned late at night with his helmet and headlight, a commuter style that impressed everyone. He wore it as a conversation badge. "Yes, I ride my bike to and from work," he announced, especially to older people, and waited for the inevitable disbelief. Tom liked to be a harbinger of things to come.

Way inside myself, I was torn. From the very beginning, I'd felt that Tom knew what one needed to know and that he would take me along. However, beneath the comfort of believing that I was associated with someone "in the know," wedged way under, was the cold scary thought that what Tom knew didn't matter. When I saw Tom from a distance, his long thin hair hanging as he peered, stiff-necked, repeatedly, side to side, I thought that for an adventurer, he was awfully cautious. I didn't want to think about what I felt when I saw his thick legs pumping and pumping at the pedals.

I had begun teaching English classes at a local high school. In the late afternoons, when I returned to the empty apartment where the refrigerator hummed, low and menacing, I took an aspirin and heated canned mushrooms in hot butter. Then I piled them, brown and gruesome, onto a plate. Tom would not return for hours, since his work data was sent from different time zones, late at night. The light in the living room/dining room/study was a dim light that illuminated

the dust that collected on desk legs and in uncarpeted corners. My desk, the one from my old bedroom, was narrow
with white knobs, a girl's desk. I ate there, one hand on the
plate to balance it, one hand on the piles of student papers,
trying not to notice the residue of the mushrooms. Often,
after I'd finished the mushrooms, and because my headache
had not departed, I burst into tears.

Sometimes then, I walked far into the Rock Creek neighborhood, leaning against the wind, looking for some object,
something to adore, and finding only blocks of garden apartments without gardens, short beige buildings inhabited by
widowed ladies and widowed men. My parents lived just
two miles away, but by mutual resistance our two households
were distant. It wasn't that Polina and Leonard actually said
that they didn't like Tom.

Once a week, I visited a local beautician, as Polina did.
I listened to the other women at the salon. I watched, suspended in my brown dress with the wide patent-leather belt.
I watched the sisters who always came in the same day I did,
with their duplicate rounded noses, their broad soft shoulders wedged into squared jackets. They were both married
to guys named Joe; both had wedding rings and big engagement rings squeezing their fleshy fingers. They seemed to
have everything in common. I twirled my own ring on my
finger. It was a thin, brushed gold band with small circle holes
cut into it. It looked like a little stream of gold meandering
between river rocks. It seemed spacious, as if there would
be room in marriage. I'd smiled at Tom when we picked it,

and told him that it was like a brook. He had smiled back, pleased. The ring was less than thirty dollars.

"Wedding rings are not supposed to have holes," Leonard said, as he examined it close up, "especially not cracks, for God's sake."

"Oh, Daddy," I had said, remembering for a second the sense that I was less conventional than my father, "it's a river. The crack is just like sedimentation shifting." I was pleased to have had some of the terminology of my college geology class come to mind, though I wasn't sure what I meant. Then, quickly, I came up with the notion that marriage must be about layers accruing and things moving inevitably but comfortably. The explanation seemed to satisfy everyone. Now I twirled the ring again, loose on my finger. The sisters were chortling about something, about Liz Taylor's remarriage to Richard Burton. I didn't care about Liz Taylor. What made me feel so different? So alone? Was it the words crowded thick in my head in their cocoons that prevented me from even imagining that I was part of the same species as the sisters or even Mabel, the beautician, with her mound of yellow frosted curls?

"We'd love to have hair like yours," one of the sisters usually said about my thick brown curly hair. Theirs was thin. I never knew what to say.

# *parade*

Once, we invited my parents to our apartment. There was snow on the ground, but the apartment was warm enough. Tom, recovering from flu, was home. Leonard and Polina arrived wearing sunglasses. I knew that my parents wore sunglasses when they were worried that they might reveal emotion at hospitals or funerals. I tried to explain to myself that they were protecting their eyes from the snow glare, as Jackie Kennedy did in photos, but that didn't account for wearing the glasses inside. I served tea and the cheese that they had sent for the holidays. I tried to do it right, but everything seemed insufficient. Not wanting to use my new best china for a simple afternoon snack, which would incur my mother's disdain, I chose the plastic plates Leonard had won years before from a gas station. The plates had three pandas on them. The gouda with its stiff wax covering seemed disconnected from the plates, plunked there without context. Leonard was wedged into a rocking chair

I'd found discarded on the street. Polina was sloped in a "too soft" sofa and demanded the straight-backed chair. Tom, perched unyieldingly on a kitchen chair, wore a goofy smile. I wondered if he still had a fever. He was wearing a terry cloth robe, which revealed an embarrassingly long stretch of leg. I knew he shouldn't be entertaining Leonard and Polina so casually dressed.

"So how's the job going, Tom?" Leonard asked in a bored voice.

"Fabulous," said Tom, crossing his long naked legs the other way. He'd answered with too much confidence. "I should probably get a raise next review. We've got a new computer-assisted analysis product coming by spring. Should mean a bonus." Tom grinned his soft glad blue-and-white smile.

"No," I screamed silently, "you don't parade good fortune that hasn't even occurred. Underplay it; they'll cream you." I escaped to the kitchen to get a knife for the cheese.

# 1970

# self-congratulation

I t was the picture of the bleak islands, black against the
sky, in the *New York Times* travel section that drew Tom to
Norway. Tom had determined to go up the coast of Norway
all the way to the Lofoten Islands, north of the Arctic Circle,
but I hadn't heard about that detail yet. I was amazed at
Tom's idea of going anywhere, much less to Norway for three
weeks in July. I'd never have thought of Scandinavia, having
no associations with it, though I realized that tall blond Tom
must identify with the pale isolation of the north, with the
Norsemen, perched on rock edges, living without comforts.
Tom seemed dedicated to austerity.

Our first evening in Bergen was cool and gray. Tom had
whitefish for dinner, with white potatoes.

"I've been thinking," Tom announced. "I've been thinking about money, about how differently we spend it." I was
instantly on the alert. This wasn't what I expected him to be
thinking about.

"I have a proposal," Tom added, being responsible, as always. "So I won't have to feel annoyed or even know what you are buying, how about if we split our incomes right down the middle. Half each. We can split our joint expenses likewise. Every month we'll tally up what each has spent for the joint household and reimburse each other for whatever is not balanced. Then the rest is each of ours to spend or not, however we want."

"Oh," I answered, carefully. "I guess that seems fair."

I hadn't realized he was annoyed. I'd thought I'd been pretty economical, but maybe buying any clothes at all seemed excessive to him. Maybe it was excessive. This plan of his did give me some room, some space I hadn't realized I wanted. What a bold, flexible plan, I decided—so unconventional, so appropriate.

When Tom said that he really wanted to get above the Arctic Circle, take the train up the coast to those islands he read about, I realized that I didn't. In fact, nothing could have been less appealing to me at that moment than trekking farther north, toward more bleakness.

"Well, why don't I go north and you south?" Tom proposed when I hesitated. We agreed where we would meet, in Oslo, in a week.

Far from striking either one of us as odd that we were taking separate trips on our first vacation together, we were impressed with our mutual and remarkable flexibility. Why not honor each one's needs in this way that impeded neither? How were we to understand the extent to which our ingenious plan indicted us?

When I woke the next day, I decided where I would go. It was my first time reading a map and considering my options since my trip, three years before, through Marseille to Israel. There was something familiar about the possibility of spontaneity. There on the map was Kristiansund, the southernmost end of the railroad line. That was where I'd go. I wanted to see white summer cottages, domesticity, women in colored scarves hanging wash, the possibility of babies' skin. Yes, I'd flee the brooding northern darkness—go south, to yellow.

It felt wonderful to be by myself on the train with its quaint wooden corridors and window frames. Since I couldn't speak the language, I felt mysterious. With each mile, I felt myself melting, my cheeks getting softer, my lips tasting sweeter—like berries, like soft seedy raspberries dripping red and rich in my released mind. I became simply a woman on a train south to summer, heading for the closest version of Mediterranean I could accomplish.

I arrived in Kristiansund at noon and hopped off the train with my small backpack and sneakers. Unbelievably, I hadn't actually planned beyond "south." I hadn't thought about what I would do or where I might stay. I walked past a few summer stalls set up near the train station, and bought a soft yellow jersey to commemorate the trip. It was cheap and, anyway, it was my money now to do with as I wanted. Then, fingering the jersey with pleasure, I sat at a little café for coffee and a roll and butter in the thin but real sun, and a thought arrived in my mind. That was the wonder of it then.

First nothing, then, a thought: *Well, now I know what to do. I've come south and got what I wanted, now I'll follow Tom. I'll follow him north.*

I took the train north from Kristiansund. Since so little time had passed between my arrival and my new plan, it was literally the same train, the same porters from the train south. So, grins exchanged, and now in the thin patterned jersey, I sat looking out the other side of the train to ride back. There was only the one route, straight up the coast. *Ah*, I thought, again, *I will stop in all the spots Tom has said he would see and thus have random information to throw into conversations in the future, to mystify him.* He'd never know how I knew. I planned not to tell him I'd done anything but travel south. The audacity of my plan thrilled me.

I didn't investigate why having an untraceable source of knowledge seemed so empowering. There, suddenly and blessedly, seemed to be no other options to consider, since Tom had carved a path. I was simultaneously freed of the necessity to choose and self-congratulatory about my inventiveness.

## *the ease with which I might*

There was one particular stop I made in Trondheim, at a music museum. I knew Tom planned to see the museum, so when I learned that the public transport was on strike, I spent extra money to take a taxi. Alone there, I wandered into a room full of violins. Violins of all sorts, real and invented, were everywhere, on the walls, on the floors, heaped in corners, piled on chairs. There was one made entirely of nails. I was sure Tom would be impressed with this extensive variation on a theme.

The next room was a mock-up of Chopin's dark rehearsal room. George Sands, in wax, leaned over a piano, where a wax Chopin sat. Their long white fingers swooned together over the keyboard. Alone in the room, I was transfixed by their grace.

Coming back into the white light of the main hall, I encountered a stream of people speaking English. They were a British touring group transported to the museum on their British tour bus. Only they, in their independent vehicle, and I, emboldened to traverse the countryside in a taxi, had arrived at the museum all day. I was invited to join them at a luncheon set up for the tour in a back room of the museum. We feasted on dark bread, rich cheese, and bits of salted herring. Who was I, I wondered, a married child among these middle-aged adults, drifting and certain in some buoyant current? They offered me a ride back in their bus, to the train station.

Late that night, I resumed the train ride that deposited me at Böde, the last point before the boat to the Lofotens. Amazingly, the boat turned out to be the same boat the English tourists were taking. Like a princess in a dream, each of my steps was creating the next scene. I recognized a familiar sensation when a couple invited me to shower in their cabin, left me freely in their room, and departed with offers of: "Here, have this soap. Here, take some chocolate our daughter-in-law gave us dock-side. Here, we don't need it, enjoy it, sorry we can't invite you to the dinner, they count us carefully. Here, dear."

They'd listened to the story of my secret pursuit of my husband with enthusiasm. "I am going to surprise him by knowing all these things, like about the museum." I, floating up, up to my husband, must have seemed an interesting diversion, an American invention.

I recognized their response from an acting class I'd taken in college. It was called The Clown. The woman who taught it had studied mime in Paris with Marcel Marceau and believed that each student had within them, buried in a protected pod, a Clown.

"A hidden signature of yourself, often at odds with the image you try to project," she said.

Before that class, I thought I had my teachers and my peers completely fooled. I walked to and from classes purposefully. How were they to know that I just liked hearing my heels click on sidewalks or in halls, that the echoing stride reminded me of Polina moving through the world as if it were hers to move through?

To my amazement, in an earlier class, I'd been cast in a play as a madam in a brothel in Nazi Germany. I'd been costumed in black, with black fingernails and black lips. Silver sequins arrayed my eyes and body; a black whip was thick in my right hand, a black wide cigar in my mouth. It was a speechless part. As I'd shifted my way sinuously through the cabaret scene, I crooned quietly to myself, *they see me as even more menacing than I imagined.* I flaunted my hips and grinned inwardly behind my dark mouth.

But the clowning class undid me, for slowly my Clown began to emerge. It came through when the external material was stripped off, like a sculpted piece. The final for the class involved exposure to the outside world. We were to dress our Clown in the clothes it required and meet at a two-block area on a Friday afternoon. Our teacher would move from spot to spot, noting the reaction of people to the Clowns. I thought that meant she would see if we stayed in character. I'd decided that my Clown, in its outer manifestation, was a Pittsburgh waitress. She was pale, stiff, with white fleshy arms. Her yellow hair would be straight and uniform. (I'd found just the wig: soft, dull.) My Clown waitress had barely made it through high school and now was out, at last. I borrowed the perfect mustard-colored uniform with a small white apron for the Friday class. It was perfectly a little too tight across my hips. I painted her fingernails a pale pearly pink. One nail smudged. I wore old white tennis shoes over too-light stockings. I knew that even though in ordinary life I always walked to the university briskly, past the large and gardened old faculty houses, my waitress would never choose to walk. And being forced to walk, she would walk slowly and without energy.

By the time I, as my Clown, mounted the bus and quietly, so I was asked to speak up, asked for a transfer to "Donton," Pittsburghese for downtown, I knew that something had happened to me.

Friday afternoon, on the two blocks in question, was prime time, Happy Hour for the frat houses and the medical students at the university. That Friday afternoon of the Clown class, I lost sight of my classmates. Walking slowly down the main street, I felt an old lethargy sweep up my legs and a quiet meadow envelop me. I didn't know where I was going, released thus, suddenly, by the class assignment, from my usual hasty and purposeful progress. I walked slowly, dumbly, while laughing students parted to pass, without comment, around me. Only the sight of the teacher halfway down the block kept me hooked to any line at all. It seemed as if, lacking that lifeline, I might have melted on the spot, drizzled down to a heap of pink and mustard. In a while, though, even the teacher faded into the crowd.

Just this side of panic, I returned sufficiently to physical awareness to notice a great hole of thirst parching my throat. I directed my heavy feet into a local store.

"Coke, please," I said in a new thin reedy voice.

"No coke, only Pepsi," the large dark-haired boy said, looking in a rather concentrated way at me.

For my Clown, every word was a bridge constructed under extreme hardship. I reached into her silky-sounding rayon pocket and pulled out, along with some hairs and bits of napkin balls, twelve cents. "Oh dear," I said, halfway between personalities, staring at the clerk who hushed me.

"Don't worry, it's OK, I'll give you one," he said.

It grew hotter and crowded in the wig. After a while, my Clown sought relief, any dark room. The nearest was a bar. When I entered, a few people were scattered about in groups. My Clown sought only creature comforts, only the dark corner under the black ceiling. I sat on a chair and noticed, then, the teacher again, lurking at the doorway, clearly though unaccountably pleased. My Clown was content to sit. But before long, a medical student dressed in blue hospital scrubs approached.

"Here," he said, sympathetically, "why don't you have the rest of this pizza. We're done."

My Clown sat silently munching very very slowly the cool but welcome pizza, her needs attended to by patient, solicitous, and infinitely wise humans. Then, sated, I joined the milling crowd.

At the end of the class, the teacher, barely able to contain herself, boasted about the amazing success of my dear Clown. My Clown had waited within me for my manipulations to cease for me to realize the ease with which I might float upon the beneficence of the world.

So I was not surprised by what happened in Norway. I'd had the experience of unasked-for gifts, of my presence causing people to help me, of things just working out. It certainly wasn't Tom's way. His was to work a problem to its solution. He could, and did, feel that he'd earned everything he had.

I'd decided that my Clown was not to be used often, not on purpose, not to be used up or taken advantage of, since it wasn't really fair that I got things without working, was it? That was what I'd learned from Tom.

After the send-off gifts to me, or my Clown, of perfume and more chocolates, I left the British tourists and walked down the gangplank onto the largest of the Lofoten Islands.

The island looked bleak, anticlimactic. Unbelievably, since it was August, there was still snow, thawing slowly, in cool puddles. Fish hung stiff and dry on the ramshackle cottage walls over peeling green paint. Makeshift plank bridges stretched from island to island. Once again I had made no plans for arrival.

# a hole to fish through

I wandered down the only street into an office with a tourism insignia on the door. The room looked more like the waiting station of an auto repair shop than a tourist bureau. There were a few old maps on the desk; on the walls were faded pictures of wooden churches and some fish-smelling rags near the door. A young man wearing a white shirt and black pants, so not a fisherman but a government agent, looked up from a desk.

"Um, room? Hotel?" I said.

The tourist agent laughed stiffly at my attempt. He was clearly not used to English-speaking tourists. I hardly knew how to form a question. How long was I planning to stay? What kind of place was there here, and what would I do all day? Not to mention the cost, though it couldn't cost that much. I'd been so preoccupied by the notion of the trip and then the amusement of being taken for my Clown that the sudden drop to hard literal existence was a bit of a jolt.

"Bed here, one night, twenty." The young man pointed to some writing. Under the column marked dollars was indeed the number twenty. It was a single room with a bathroom, even.

"Yes, good. Yes," I said.

The young man pointed down the street to a faded red building. "There, yah?" he said.

"Good."

But I didn't leave yet. I wanted a little more of a plan but didn't know how to ask. I saw a little bus trademark on the bottom of a poster of a wooden church. That was the kind of thing Tom might do, take an organized tour, get the lay of the land. That was what I'd try. After all, I dimly remembered, the whole point was to duplicate Tom's trip, right?

"When is the next bus to the churches? Vikings?"

I felt a little idiotic. I was asking about the bus, slowly trying to stretch out this connection with someone, who, if only because it was his employment, was bound to consider with me the nature of my days.

Suddenly, the door opened. The young man looked up again. I turned, and there was Tom. At first, oddly, I didn't register that it was unusual to see him. Then I realized that he didn't seem surprised to see me. Nor glad. We walked toward each other and embraced, silently. I revolved around to the tourist agent, thinking that he'd be stunned at my sudden acquaintance, since I'd obviously come in alone.

Tom didn't want to alter his living arrangement for the posh extravagance of my newly acquired room. He showed me his dwelling place. He was sharing a room in one of the fishing cottages right over the water with an old Norseman and a Japanese couple who followed a special diet of only indigenous morsels—so it was potatoes and fishes in abundance. Tom was quite taken with the notion. There were two holes on the wharf outside his sleeping quarters. One was for the men in winter, to urinate through, splashing down to the sea. One was to fish through, dragging a line in the water first thing, probably at three in the morning.

# 1974

## a paradise, sort of

With only an undergraduate degree, but with honors and work experience under his belt, Tom was offered a choice between three job opportunities. We could move to Northampton, Massachusetts; Madison, Wisconsin; or Los Angeles. I imagined the bright yellow trees in Massachusetts, then snow over the rivers and through the woods. Madison, though I'd never been there, seemed like cool milk. A mist on some farmland, frost crunching underfoot, a solid coldness. LA seemed by far the most exotic, the most unlikely to come to us again, the most unimaginable. So that's where we moved.

Tom took a job on the faculty of Los Angeles City College. Though he was the youngest, most junior member of the faculty, he'd been named head of the department. The position involved negotiating between various professors who wanted the few rooms with windows. Tom dedicated himself to being fair. The other professors all had side jobs that brought them extra money (and probably were not interested in the status of chairman). It wasn't like a high school English department; there was money to be made off-campus.

Tom was dutiful, there from nine to five and after. Also he'd been helping a woman named Pat who had her degree in art and was the department secretary.

"Poor Pat," Tom clucked, sympathetically, "she works so hard and they treat her so badly, loading her up with documents right at closing time."

The house we bought was on Floraciente Street. I was ecstatic that camellias bloomed in our own backyard. There were two bushes full, one, a soft slated pink, its face pushed flat in neatly ordered discs. The birds of paradise erupted not just once, but twice a year. The roses bloomed and bloomed, multiple times. I witnessed the arrival of the aphids and tried different techniques of removal. I sprayed them with poison. Then, as I became more environmentally aware, I sprayed them with detergent. The methods were equally ineffective. Some weeks, I squished the little aphids, determined to save the roses' suffering. They went on blooming, gigantic blossoms, yellow tinged in pink, each lasting only one glorious day. I decked the little house with them. Roses were in the living room, on the window ledges, in the kitchen, even in the bathroom, on the bathtub.

In California, I was a child again, content to drift for hours gazing at the bouquets from the backyard's generosity. I watched into the long slow afternoons the seaward flight of gulls to sunset. I'd learned from Otis and Emily next door that the previous owner of the house had sat naked in the backyard with her cello. Otis and Emily both grew up in Nebraska, had worked in the aerospace industry, and were now retired. Otis still wore overalls and Emily gingham aprons, as if in costume for a Depression-era movie. They watered their tomatoes, hung towels on the clothesline, and spoke to their cats. I imagined Polina's distaste. Polina couldn't abide it if an adult let a child interrupt a conversation: how she would dislike the reign of the cats. But way out here, all these miles and mountains from anything I had known, those rules seemed upside-down. The fecundity of the place forbade the narrow judgments and dismissals of my parents' world. Too much was in motion here to claim a static truth. The earthquakes and shifting sands articulated some premise that one needed only a nimble flexibility to ride the earth.

# my own rabbi

When I first encountered Alan Hertzl, he was wearing long white robes in front of his congregation in West Hollywood. Behind him, the wall was a painted sky with white clouds. The sun came through two yellow lion windows. Rabbi Hertzl was surrounded by colorful children who swarmed the *bimah*, then settled in little groups around the edges, herded by the sun and shadows of his expression. One, in white stockings, was perched in his large chair. That was his youngest daughter, I found out later. The whole scene looked like spring; the children, portulacas, blooming.

Hertzl's white muslin robe had small buttonholes made of threads twined together in repeated loops over his chest. I noticed that his shoes were white clogs. He looked like a Venice Beach man in his ocean robes, tan with soft hair.

After the service, the women and men wandered companionably into the reception hall to eat herring and dry cakes. Women clustered, welcoming me, the stranger, with their soft faces and red lips. They knew each other from years of weddings, births, sicknesses, and deaths.

"Isn't our new rabbi wonderful?" they asked, agreeing with themselves.

"He seems amazing," I said.

"Too bad he's divorced," one, named Rose, clucked. "But, well, what can you do? It happens, eh?"

I'd never thought about a rabbi's marital status before. Never actually thought about a rabbi before as a person. In my experience rabbis were always old, unapproachable. I wasn't sure I wanted to think about Rabbi Hertzl as a man, but I was. The women continued, as if they were talking to themselves but toward me, waiting for me to agree with their delight.

"He is young! Maybe he's a little too, well, unconventional. Still . . ." Rose bit into a small almond cookie. "He's brought new life to the place. It couldn't go on like it was, all the children moving out of the city." She gestured with a crumb-covered sleeve. "He's brought you. So where do you live, dear?"

"I live just a few blocks away. I just moved to Los Angeles a few months ago."

"Welcome," said several of the women. I couldn't get over women in a city synagogue in bright flowered dresses.

"So, what brought you to this temple?" one asked. She didn't seem nosy, just interested.

"Well, I didn't really know how to choose, so I just chose the closest to start with. But when I walked in, it just seems so beautiful in here, and the rabbi looks really alive."

I didn't tell them I was looking for some link to something, some sense of my own importance, my shape in space. I hardly knew this. What I knew was that here in Los Angeles where there seemed room for anything, I'd remembered that I was Jewish. Suddenly it seemed interesting, instead of ordinary and assumed. The desert dry air had given me room to imagine.

I noticed that I'd not mentioned Tom. Partly that was because I didn't know what the reaction would be to my non-Jewish husband. But more, if I admitted it, I omitted him because I wanted this adventure to be mine alone. The next day, following up on some sense of possibility, I called Rabbi Hertzl.

"Well, yes?" his secretary, Ronit, answered, clearly intrigued by any female calling the rabbi. "What would you like? Wait a minute." There was silence, then his voice.

"Yes, this is Alan Hertzl."

"Hello," I introduced myself. "I would like a little time to talk with you." Could it possibly be so simple? In Los Angeles, it seemed as if everyone was flexible, ready to see what would happen next.

"I could see you Monday. Wednesday. Can it wait? Do I know you?" the rabbi asked. I held my voice as steady as I could, trying to figure out what I'd say next.

"I'd like to get to know you."

I found myself falling back on a familiar phrase, feeling that I thus opened the door to him, without saying too much. Really, it was true; I wanted to enter the regions of his knowledge. My offer of an exchange of interest in him was my currency for purchasing mutuality.

———

The next Wednesday, I dressed in a pastel skirt covered in light squares of yellow, scarlet, green, and turquoise, a pink sweater woven also in squares, and blue sandals. I looked like a Jewish dancer located, oddly, somewhere in Scandinavia. Not too bold, not too demure, not too old, and not too innocent. Well, maybe too innocent.

Ronit, perched behind her desk, was short. She looked up over her glasses. "The rabbi will be with you soon, he is finishing the adult class. You can wait in the lobby, I suppose you'll be able to use the hall chairs for your meeting."

Another woman in the office looked out at me from behind a typewriter. "Ronit, want some sunflower seeds?"

"Sunflower seeds?" Ronit answered. "What, are you crazy?"

I kept my attention on the black-and-white photographs hanging on the walls. In one was a picture of the rabbi, very young, everything about him too skinny. I wandered down the wall of announcements and pictures, watching the words slide by without even a tiny snag of sense. When I finally heard his steps on the hall floor, Rabbi Hertzl was moving fast.

"Are you here to see me?"

And before I responded, out loud, both of us were smiling dangerously. "I want to apologize for being late. I was at my class, but still, I'm sorry to have kept you."

"It's all right, I've been looking at these old photos. You look different." I stopped myself, not sure what to divulge. He seemed so much more physical than the pictures of him.

He was dressed all in sandy browns, brown-haired, and the blue of his eyes was striking. He gestured an apology and an assurance and walked rapidly into his office.

"Any call from Harold at Beth El? How about Samuel, is he still in intensive care?"

"No, Rabbi," Ronit answered. "But the Colemans want to talk to you about the wedding."

"Look, Ron," the rabbi said, "I'll be meeting with this young woman here, and I don't want to be disturbed unless it's an emergency."

This had all been loud enough for me to hear. I'd been walking slowly, toward the office, not wanting to rush, to look silly. When I arrived at the door, Rabbi Hertzl smiled. "How about the chapel, do you know it?" he asked.

"No, but fine." I was relieved to have him making plans for us that included privacy and not being interrupted. The chapel was just out the back door of his personal office. It was a small sunny room with an ancient-looking enclosure worked in silver where the Torah was kept. I had expected to be confronted by questions about my religious history. I was relatively ready to rush through my parents' lapsed orthodoxy, their feeble and brief attempt to send us to classes at a reform synagogue, though they lived a life devoid of religious ritual, and my subsequent, and so far unmentioned, marriage out of the faith to Tom. Then I would try to explain my journey into this temple with its light and song.

But there we sat, face-to-face, silent. His wheaten hair, my blushing heart. There had been a little pause before sitting, during which I had calculated the risks and reassurances of the possible positions on the bench.

"You tell me first," the rabbi started. "Are you married?"

Not the question I'd expected.

"Yes . . . He isn't Jewish," I added, though Hertzl hadn't asked, and besides, was that really the point?

"How long have you been married?"

"Two years," I answered, unsure now where we were going.

"Forbidden territory," the rabbi mused. "Neither fish nor fowl is the young married woman. Neither old nor single," he continued, in a soft voice, "she is forbidden. So I felt, if I felt anything, when you mentioned that you wanted to get to know me, if I felt anything—" and here he paused, head bent as if to contemplate what he had felt. The yarmulke that day was a gentle mix of beiges, blues, and sandy yellows.

I remembered, unexpectedly, an afternoon I had once spent in a Bedouin tent one summer our parents had sent Joyce and me to camp in Israel. The huge fabric mildly swaying overhead created a calm world in which the Bedouins moved, flowing in their own drapery and going about their shaded tasks, while outside the sun beat the sands.

"If I felt anything, I put it out of my mind," the rabbi finished. I laughed. The nervous strings inside my brain were bursting merrily, making pretty patterns bordering the picture in my mind of the Forbidden Territory. I stood at the edge of it, removing the warning sign, tossing it off to the side and walking, stalwartly, straight in. I noticed Hertzl's eyes glowing.

"Frankly, I was afraid when you posed the question so open-endedly. You'd like to get to know me . . ."

"Oh," I interrupted, "I didn't ask if that was all right with you. I knew that I'm trustworthy." I was aware of my lipstick, so close and slick on my lips.

"Well then. I would love to have you, and your husband, come to my house for Shabbat dinner," Hertzl announced, most unexpectedly. "Perhaps this week. I'll give you a call."

# hints of heat

I was certainly not prepared for the Shabbat dinner, not for the thick azaleas at the door and not for the other women. I realized when I saw the plants blooming by the door that I'd assumed Rabbi Hertzl had no flowers. I'd bought beautiful yellow globes of tulips. A neighbor of the rabbi's took them from me and mixed them with the forsythia already on the Shabbos table. I had also brought a tiny challah, proud of my effort at tradition.

Dressing, I had tried to strike a clear but modest tone, presuming I'd be the only woman at the event. I wore a red but long-sleeved blouse. Unfortunately, I matched one of the several other women. But the other was wearing a bright red dress cut in a shimmery V showing the round and moving shape of her breasts. This was Reva, in cocktail party heels and a mane of frisky black hair. Reva was the quintessential Jewish woman, I thought. And she even taught in Hebrew school. But maybe she was too obvious, no nuance, I hoped.

Reva followed, all evening, one little step behind the rabbi.

"Yes, he and I made the salad," Reva confided. "Yes, you're right, he's awful," she whispered with a smile between dimples, to the rabbi's oldest daughter, who scowled magnificently at the haphazard hostmanship of her wifeless father, gathering again a random sampling of assorted guests for Shabbat.

"Oh, these poor girls," Reva clucked about the rabbi's three girls, the two teenagers and the small one. "How difficult it is for him without a woman, you can see," she said. Reva cast a demonstrative gesture at the house. "It's so hard on him."

I wondered who Reva was convincing. Actually, the house was full of beautiful objects, but it did lack the loving touch that arranges things attractively.

In the kitchen, the friendly, motherly neighbor poked at a kugel. The two youngest daughters, dressed head to toe in prettiness, played a sociable half-hearted tag. I moved around, trying, in vain, to figure out what I could do. In the warm oven, heaps of chicken, and three different versions of kugel, hummed. My tiny challah was balanced over a hot plate that had someone's offering of a store-bought challah and several plates of stale matzo, which were, presumably, being crisped up to new vitality.

The last guest to arrive was Henya. She swept in, covered in layers of mauve and pastel flowers, wearing leather boots. I felt Henya's superiority as she moved past the other women in the kitchen to a counter, where she started to assemble a rigorously healthy salad. She chopped without comment, except to take offense at someone's mistaken use of her lettuce bag as a garbage bag. Just then the rabbi reappeared, dressed in an even more spectacular white robe than the first time I'd seen him. This one was embroidered in thin strands of gold thread. I felt the sudden joy of the sabbath in his approach—and wanted to cling to it. How beautiful he was, white and gold, evoking, without diminishing his manhood, the Sabbath Bride. He seemed handsomely familiar. But then, with Reva beside him, he turned rabbinical. "By the right hand of God. Why the right?" The question seemed genuine.

Henya had been seated next to me. She spent the evening throwing articulate bullets into the past, at her short-term and handily removed husband, and at her narrow but learned orthodox Toronto upbringing. Though she clearly and intelligently maligned it, she knew the religious ritual so well that she could chime in wherever the rabbi was in his ceremony without missing a note in her conversation with me. She smiled triumphantly at the rabbi, two single and successful survivors. He smiled back, then smiled around the table.

"This is a very good friend!" he introduced Henya.

I didn't know for sure if I was hearing a nuance. Henya gave me her card. It had her name in tastefully decorated letters and a slate blue phoenix design etched across the top. Her name, HENYA HYLAR, and under it, HOLISTIC PSYCHIATRY. Henya dug into the healthy salad with enormous gusto. I was defeated.

However, as I left, Rabbi Hertzl thanked me warmly for coming and suggested I come by for another conversation.

"Anytime." He winked softly as I looked back from the path.

———

A week later, I sat in on a class Alan Hertzl was teaching. One older woman strained her wrinkled neck and eked out, with great solemnity, "Now why, Rabbi, if God is so good, why is it that bad things happen to good people?"

I was startled. People were still asking that question? Did they really think the universe was so simple? Hadn't they already grappled with, and resolved, this question? Maybe the question was only for reassurance, like a child clattering a stick along a gate for the expected sound. The women in the class, and the one retired man, were maybe just echoing a question for the reassurance of the answer: the sweet familiar ring of "Yes, yes, the ancients asked that, too, and answered just as you do." Hertzl didn't really answer the question. He just dignified it.

After the class, Alan and I walked along San Vicente Boulevard with the breeze and the grass still green in early spring. Our height and stride were exactly compatible. Alan hadn't said anything yet. I certainly didn't say, "It is not your lips, it is not your sandy hair, it is your wisdom I love." This was partly because I was already, accidentally, imagining his lips.

Hertzl asked, "Now why are you so silent, so timid?"

And I, though unknown Talmudic debates waited unmouthed in my mind, replied, "But I am not, not, really not, I only seem timid, but really I'm not."

Hertzl added, "I'm a little frightened." Not even asking what he was afraid of, I reassured him.

"Now, don't be. I really just want to give you room." It seemed to me, then, that space was what I could offer that differentiated me from the other women, from Reva, who seemed to be clambering over him, from Henya who stood up to him so stridently. When Alan turned to me, he took both my hands in his. I felt that I was on the right track.

"Thank you. Thank you," he said. The winds on the boulevard seemed beautiful, gentle and graceful. We walked to a Chinese restaurant for lunch. The room was dark. There was no one else in the restaurant. I sat opposite Alan, who didn't seem to be really looking at me. His eyes simply settled in my direction as a convenient location, a familiar resting place. Then suddenly he said, "Reva is really a delightful woman. I can't tell why I hesitate."

He seemed to be asking for my assistance. Was he right in not wanting to settle down quite yet?

"Have we an agenda?" I asked after a while, hoping to change the subject.

"No," he said, "we're friends."

"Well," I started, "it was really frustrating that people in your class seemed so self-absorbed. I mean they seemed just worried about how to prevent disasters in their own lives."

I hoped he noticed my ability to get the whole picture. Alan agreed, calmly.

"Yes, they don't understand the notion of suffering."

He suggested that we walk to a park. That seemed promising, it was open-ended. Who knew what might happen? We walked in silence. A soft breeze ruffled first his, then my own hair. My feet felt delicate, as if I were walking in a dream, over flowers, holding his hand. The air had a hint of summer heat, the scent of eucalyptus. When we passed a bench, Alan yawned, and I invited him to rest. He sat, unbuttoning his top buttons and removing his tie. Then he dozed on the bench. His whole body shifted to lean against mine as he fell into a semi-sleep. Not really wanting him to sleep, I whispered to him to tell me what he saw.

"A ship," he murmured. "A ship. Trumpets." Then, a while later, "Yet I feel alone."

The rest was incoherent. He fell asleep, his sweet yet inaccessible weight leaning on me. When a half hour or so later he woke, he looked at me with serene and rested eyes. I held my breath, softly, waiting. He seemed about to kiss me.

Instead he said, "You are a mystic, a true Jewish mystic."

After my disappointment, which I tried to ignore, I was enthralled. Perhaps he had seen me, truly, and as more exalted than I even imagined. Yet where had he placed me? He'd lifted me to a special airy region where Reva did not float. He'd lifted me, in one slim sentence, beyond his reach. I felt heady and alone.

# outrage

I began to clean the house that night. Clearing the surfaces, I came to Tom's dresser. I removed several socks and an open sheet of paper. The paper was a letter from Pat, the secretary at the university, a letter about his hands on her body and what a dear he was. The letter in my hands began to flutter noisily. I walked into the living room with it and lifted it toward Tom.

"What is this? What is this?" I asked, terrified of confronting him.

He'd been napping on the living room couch, and when he turned to me and saw the letter, his face turned rigid. He raised himself from the couch in one gray block.

"How dare you read mail that is addressed to me?"

I was so surprised by his comment that I didn't know what to say. Tom repeated the question, demanding an answer. Framed that way, I didn't exactly know how I'd dared. I hadn't thought reading a page lying open on a table was a big deal. Mortified, I realized I must, again, have violated some principle understood by all right-thinking people. Why could I never think as socially conscious, moral people did?

Clearly, according to Tom, the outrage was in violating privacy. I'd broken the social contract. It was my upper middle-class entitlement, as Tom often observed, that made me think the world owed me whatever it had. I just took things. I stole dabs of hand lotion from other people's bathrooms. I peeked into my mother's hatbox.

Pat has been abused, Tom told me, by her alcoholic father. She married young to get away.

"Do you know what that's like? Everything has come easy to you."

That night in bed, I hardly moved. I just stopped, almost stopped breathing. Certainly, I tried to make no noise. When the police helicopters hovered overhead, I was grateful for the way they drowned out all other sound. I could tell Tom was awake. He seemed to be staring at the wall, still furious. I imagined his dismay, his leaving this letter on his dresser, trusting me.

Was it trust? Had I betrayed an innocent trust? That seemed awful. Heartbreaking. His good clear American trust. Had I done a similar thing with the rabbi? Had I only been saved from some terrible self-indulgence by luck, by Reva? I never thought before I acted. And Tom, had he really actually slept with Pat? That seemed unbelievable. I didn't want to imagine that scene. Tom's violent reaction to my finding the paper seemed stronger than anything else. But under it, I was amazed that Tom had had enough interest to divert himself from his work.

Tom's body was a blue marble wall.

**1983**

## *desire to flaunt*

When Tom left the academic world for a more lucrative job in a company in Boston, he hadn't exactly admitted that they'd been taking advantage of him, instead he told me that there was a new actuarial firm in Boston, not so far from the Cape Cod I'd loved as a child. I liked the idea of motion. It was refreshing to contemplate novelty after the predictable years of growing up.

We moved from our little house in LA to a sturdy colonial that was a version of my parents' house in miniature. I knew where everything went from the first day I entered it. There was even a small laundry room, painted pink, in the basement and a large sunroom, though on the other side of the house than the one at my parents' with its filtering bamboo shades. The shades had seemed to absorb the heavy, humid Washington air and to release dry lengths of sun and shadow cutouts on the floor. In late afternoon the shades were rolled up, and the long French windows opened. By twilight, the crickets screamed through them. Polina and Leonard would invite friends for drinks and cribbage matches. I remembered the laughing and cigarettes, card tables, tan legs, and exultant words. Everyone sat on tight-weave chairs made of reed, which scraped sunburned skin pleasantly. They ate peanuts, leaving the shells in little pottery bowls that matched the rug. The smoke and enthusiasm of their conversations drifted out of the screened porch. Polina wore large Mexican skirts and tidy embroidered cotton blouses.

We'd only lived in our own new house for seven months when Pat arrived in March. She was cold all the time. She came to breakfast in sweatpants and one of Tom's jackets. When Tom asked me if Pat could come, his face had looked like tissue paper, transparent and flammable. I was frightened. We had just finished eating warm apple pie, and I was feeling proud of my domestic accomplishment.

"So," Tom had said, as if about to chat with me in the amiable way I envied in other couples, "it looks like Pat has decided to try around Boston for a job. She isn't having any luck in Kentucky." I had swallowed and swallowed again, the cinnamon suddenly thickening in my throat. "I want to offer her our house while she looks for a job and a place to live. Do you have a problem with that?"

Tom was way ahead of me. I had worried about Pat being in the same town. In our own house was at first offensive and then, suddenly, preferable. I could keep an eye on her. Yes, I could prove, at last, that I could handle even that. But my eyes blurred. Tom stared. It was a test.

"Yes, she can," I said, trying to sound confidently casual.

Still, it was a surprise when Pat moved in: herself, her things, and her little dog. She took over the guest room and found places for her pots and pans in the kitchen. The dog was put in the basement. I insisted on that. It was a puppy, and ordinarily, I would have wanted its small beastliness near. But now, when I went down to the basement to do laundry, I ignored its furry and whining entreaties. The dog's response was to defecate, concisely, in every corner of the basement. Pat noticed and started washing the entire basement floor every few days. Until her arrival, it had never even been swept. By unspoken agreement, I did not refer to the extra work this represented. The taste of my unexpressed rage was like stale metal in my mouth.

Pat used the expensive paring knife to chop cabbage into sharp slim strips, her eyes focused to the task. *Frenetic*, I thought. *Jab jab jab*. "See, I can eat all I want of this stuff," Pat explained. She'd recently joined Weight Watchers. Apparently, after we left, she'd married a childhood boy-friend, who took her to Kentucky, where they lived in a lonely rural house. He was rarely home with her, and she'd gained a lot of weight. After a while, she left him. Now, she consumed huge mouthfuls of vegetable strips, even as she chopped. Pat's permitted selected morsels, four ounces of this, two tablespoons of that—the calculations, the joy-denying restrictions were pathetic. *I am for mounds*, I thought, heaps of rich cheese, for instance.

I couldn't account for this desire to flaunt in front of Pat. I opened a bag of peanuts right in front her and munched them all. I toasted thick slices of seven-grain bread and

spread them warmly with butter. I walked right in the door;
it was after all my house, not Pat's. It was not Pat's house,
even though Pat had moved all her possessions into it and
had been there for two weeks, with no end in sight. I walked
right in and greeted Pat in the kitchen.

"Pat, what do you think of this skirt?" I was aware that
I was flaunting the fact that I could buy it and Pat couldn't.
But it never worked. Pat, without envy, took me up on the
question.

"It is such a nice color. Now you probably need a soft
linen blouse, maybe apricot with puffy little sleeves." So
demure she was, as she looked down at her cabbage, bit-
ing at one or two strips, virtuously. She took stage by this
absence of anger. It made me glare at Tom, who had just
come in from work and was watching Pat.

"What do you mean you haven't gotten the groceries; I
told you this morning that I was tired of doing all the shopping!" I heard myself barking at Tom. I was caught between
outrage and shame. And even though I knew it was unim-
portant, all of it, I felt compelled to continue. Knowingly,
taking the risk, I moved Tom out of the kitchen with one of
those gestures that communicates quite clearly its intent. I
knew that Pat would then take over. She would have dinner,
a Weight Watcher–approved meal, all done by the time we
returned. But it was that or argue in front of her.

"Can't you hear me trying to stop those discussions?" I
begged, once we were out of earshot, in the sunroom.

"It's important to bring things out," Tom said, "Pat will
not be glad if her presence makes you cower."

"Cower? Does she say that?" I was furious.

Those days every moment quivered with deeper disaster. Still, I was lured to the edge. "How dare she say I cower, Tom, how dare she?" But what I couldn't quite articulate was that somehow the conversation had shifted from what I was feeling to how to make Pat most comfortable.

"She doesn't say that. Really, I'm getting bored with your whining. Pat is just trying to help while she is here."

I stared at him, stopped, perhaps, by the reminder that Pat would leave sometime. He was tall, commanding in the late afternoon tree-filled shadow on the floor. I could see it move, though not hear it rustle. Pat's country music station was on, deprived of full volume, gutted, all to please me. How was it that I was cast as the villain, when I felt so helpless?

Tom reminded me (it felt a lot like a reprimand), "Pat has nowhere else to go to put her life together." He was waiting. He was waiting for me to reach out of myself, to lift myself out of the quagmire I dwelt in, this ridiculous unwarranted jealousy. I must let Pat live here. Pat had nowhere else.

"Succeed," Tom said. This, I felt, was a gauntlet.

Back in the kitchen, to make up for any inconvenience she caused, Pat presented us with chicken cooked in lemon juice, a bowl of cold beans, a plate of salad with all the pieces cut, sharp-edged, into little squares, including the lettuce. For dessert, Pat presented a diet cherry Jell-O and Cool Whip with artificial sweetener. Pat looked at Tom while she scooted the nicely cut bits of food into her mouth and asked Tom to tell her about his day. He was jolly, telling her. I never asked. If I had, I feared, I would never have heard such a cheery answer. Only regret, only protestations about how boring his job was, and my work, as an underpaid substitute teacher, such a luxury.

"Tom, can we look for an apartment for me this weekend?" Pat asked, merrily.

"Of course we can, but you don't need to rush, give yourself a weekend, at least, to adjust to the move."

"Well, I don't want to impose on you."

"Don't worry, we're fine," Tom assured her without looking at me.

Pat and Tom were gone all day Saturday, looking for a home for Pat. I spent the day brushing off all the surfaces of the furniture and rearranging closets. I understood that I was trying to dust down to some clarity, but I couldn't keep my attention fixed on a single area. The dog alternately howled and scratched the basement door in a maddened attempt to escape.

## meanwhile . . .

The summer after I left for college, Polina had had air-conditioning installed in her bedroom. It began to take over rooms, one at a time. After the bedroom, an opening was sliced into the walls of Leonard's maroon study. Another air conditioner was slipped in. The wall now contained a roaring machine, which made the very air distant. The sunroom windows were closed, the bamboo shades lowered for the last time. An air-conditioning unit was installed down near the floor. Gumwood chests and chairs "from the Orient" replaced the old woven chairs. The new chairs had low-slung, smooth-as-silk mahogany feet. And where the matted woven grassy rug had lain, simple, flat upon the floor, where Polina's painted toenails in flat leather sandals from Provincetown had slapped, all this was replaced by a thick snowy white rug from the high wild sheep hills of Afghanistan.

I noticed that Polina and Leonard had moved out of the sunroom in the summer and into the cool maroon retreat that held the lively TV. I noticed Leonard's expanding belly and my mother's increasingly sharp tongue. Polina said Leonard looked like a Buddha. Polina did not know much about Buddhas and could not understand how anyone could admire a being with a belly. She dismissed the worshippers with the worshipped.

"Look at that belly. It's as fat as yours, Leonard. Maybe you should spend some time contemplating it, maybe a little soul-searching would help."

"I do look at it, and I find it superb." He'd smiled.

Polina was exasperated. But the joke continued. Polina laughed about the "pregnant" Buddha. Their friends, who were always on the lookout for a way to get Leonard to smile with pleasure, a way to meet with the red-lipped approval of Polina, took this indication of her propensity toward a kind of humor as permission.

No one bought ties for Leonard anymore since they did not hang straight down in the twentieth-century American line to the slim belt of men but, after a short descent, lifted off and curved out away, rounding the great curve of him. Leonard dealt with his protruding front by unbuttoning his shirts down past the hairy part of his upper chest and over the dark brown round of his powerful stomach.

The Buddhas began to roll in. Each gift was of the laughing Buddha with a round low belly and a satisfied smile. There was a brass one, one of rose quartz, and a jade green Buddha. Buddhas with soft pear smiles formed a merry row across Leonard's desk on the windowsill. It was not evident that Leonard took much notice of them. Extracted wholly from their heritage, they graced his thickly painted window-sill, summer and winter, still and jovial. They should have meant serenity and instead meant self.

I couldn't quite decide if Leonard's habits were getting worse since I'd left home or whether I just hadn't noticed before. What seemed new was that Leonard did not actually eat dinner or any meal at mealtimes. He chewed meat, then spat it out. He hardly took any vegetable. And I overheard him, several times, comparing notes with one of his brothers, speaking with increasing reverence of the kasha varnishkes of his mother, of the melt-in-your-mouth briskets.

"What are you talking about, Leonard?" Polina would shout from her end of the table, obviously infuriated that he seemed to prefer that overcooked cheap meat of his childhood to the fancy cuts she ordered from Magruder's Groceries. He'd grin, and I would wonder if he was egging Polina on. But none of it really mattered as long as I could still meet Leonard in the kitchen late late at night. Now we both seemed to feel we could "steal" food more openly than we had in our earlier forays.

"How's the pie?" I'd ask, coming down from the guest room where Tom would already be sleeping.

"Pretty good," Leonard would answer, and wink as he finished some lemon meringue pie and put the smeared plate in the sink.

I had always washed my late-night dishes and returned them to the cabinets so "no one would know." There was something liberating about the flagrant display of used plates.

But mostly, life seemed static at my parents' home. There were arguments in the hot summer nights. Maybe Polina went to bed early and alone more often, while Leonard sprawled in his den watching late-night TV. Still, on the tennis court, he showed up in fresh white shoes. His dark hair shone on his head. He still looked good in photos.

When Leonard started walking more slowly, Polina blamed it on his flat feet. She blamed it on his "peasant" father, the shorter left foot, the twisted spine he'd inherited. Polina had contempt for twist and deformity. It was perhaps his added weight that slowed him, that made him stop under the rose bower and pant "like a woman in labor," she'd say, when all they were doing was walking into their own house on flat land.

"Leonard, what's the matter with you? You should have that looked at," Polina would bark. She didn't say this because she actually expected that there was a cause but to threaten him with her awareness of deformity, to shock him into abandoning his growing laziness. His laziness, his weight, must have frightened her. To me, it sounded as it always had between them.

For a whole year, Polina drove Leonard, the large and often truculent body of him. And that had been bad enough with his impatient instructions.

"Pass him, goddamn it!" he'd bellow. "Turn the wheels in to the curb when you park. Now do it! Now!"

But now he just rode, inert, in the car, staring at the construction signs, the familiar apartments, the new shopping centers, the square buildings, which had been his guideposts on the way to work for forty years. Polina drove him, hor-ror-struck at the silence.

"Leonard! Leonard!" Polina demanded, trying to jump-start him out of complacency. "What are you looking at?" But his name had no harsh sound in it, no powerful consonants. The most Polina could do was push out the syllables with wind around them. It was unnerving to see my mother's fury so ineffective.

# be fair now

Once he was diagnosed with cancer, Leonard declined rapidly. One day, after a few weeks of radiation, Polina came into his den, and Leonard was counting methodically. He was up to thirty-one. His hands were folded over his chest. His belt was buckled on the tightest hole. He had stopped eating a week before. How ironic, I thought, that now Polina was cajoling him to eat.

At last, the years of excess weight were sifting, effortlessly, away. His eyes became glassy and internal. Polina tried to tempt him back to all his old indulgences. Steak, potatoes dripping with yellow butter, French fries, even pizza—all remained untouched. He was a new kind of god, self-sufficient and needing no sustenance from her. Finally, in desperation, she brought the Snickers bar that was kept frozen in the locked-up freezer in past years' attempts to keep him away from chocolate. She put it awkwardly on one of the green plates, as if it were a kind of food. The night nurse defrosted it, cut it into bite-sized pieces, and served it to him.

Leonard's eyes passed over it without interest. The dross of food was no longer a concern. His face had lost muscle tone and gone soft. His lips were flaccid. He wore his blue or his red long johns. He insisted on these, his face slack so the jowls swayed when he refused other offers. Occasionally, he did not object to his white sweater being draped over his collapsed shoulders by some attending nurse who believed that his incessant shivering reflected the weather, not his attempt to shake the frightening pieces of his life into sense before departing. That's what I thought.

Polina couldn't sleep. All day she climbed up and down the stairs, then sat in the small room that had been designated her study. It contained her medical books, her knitting, and her very large TV, which was on, loudly, almost all the time. She smoked ashtrays full of cigarettes and made phone calls to the specialists: the oncologist, the cardiologist, the internist and his associates, in a weary, demoralized voice. Her own shoulders became bony and drooping. She called Leonard's dentist, who came out to the house to attend to his teeth. She called his eye doctor who charged exorbitantly for the exam and ordered new lenses, though Leonard was not reading anymore.

Each time she entered Leonard's room full of flowers from well-wishers, Polina was met with "a cipher," or with "a ranting idiot." That's how she described it. As soon as she walked in, she scowled. Leonard sat silent. Sometimes he then spoke so eloquently, so simply, in nursery school simplicity that he seemed to me to have the wisdom of a Shakespearean fool.

"Be now, be fair. Be fair now," Leonard intoned. To me, sitting near him in the room, the request made sense. I saw that Polina's very entrance was an accusation. Someone had sold her a bill of goods, someone had betrayed her. Leonard had been uncannily accurate in voicing the issue of fairness. It wasn't just that Polina was attacking the nurse: "Don't put that ridiculous sweater on him again. It isn't cold!" It wasn't just that Leonard might be seen to be defending the nurse, finally, after all the years of ignoring Polina's sharp attacks on the household servants. It wasn't even just that Polina must have been feeling cheated by Leonard's sudden and utter deflation. All that power, his rugged dense physique, his alacrity with language, all mollified. His unfortunate years of unappealing avoirdupois, suddenly receding but too late and not even out of willpower and discipline, which would have reflected well on both of them. But it was that she was not being fair to him, not allowing him to widen out to a broader view before death. That's what I thought, as my father repeated and repeated himself sagely.

"Leonard, cut it out, you are talking nonsense. No one is being unfair to you!"

Polina spoke in an unequal mixture of fury and pity. And Leonard yelled back with fervor. "You have not been fair."

My mother would not wait on Leonard in the waking hours when he demanded a particular blue pen that was impossible to find, or the phone. (The phone was off limits. He might do damage to his own estate.) As Polina had always maintained, she never waited on Leonard. She never even waited on us children when we were babies. She would not bring him the brown towel, or the white, to put, just so, behind his head.

She did call the hospital to complain to the doctors and was told that all his reactions were typical of whatever drug he was taking. Polina's Merck's manual was marked up, the pages filled with tags locating each drug Leonard ingested and justifying the departure into a language Polina could not tolerate. She shrieked into the phone.

"You know perfectly well that Leonard is paranoid. Can't we try another approach?" This, after hearing Leonard explain to the nurse that "the life of the world is planted within us. Torah, Torah."

The nurse could not speak English very well. Polina was incensed that this hired nurse would assume that she, Polina, had married a man who ambled in this unfocused way into gardens they had left together half a century ago.

I was sure that was what my mother felt.

"He's out of his mind again," Polina told the nurse pointedly, in front of Leonard who looked up at her, sweetly. She was trying, by dint of rudeness, to create a reality she could recognize.

# *what to say*

Leonard just stopped breathing," Polina learned by phone. A doctor friend of theirs, in the hospital room at the time, called her. Polina's cry was the classic wail of a widow. The sound sliced through all the rooms of the house, cutting so sharply it was as if no blood could come to the surface.

I sat on my bed silently, listening. Joyce gasped and ran upstairs to her room sobbing. Polina slammed the door to her room. I called Tom, so he would come to Washington for the funeral the next day.

"I am so sorry," he said.

"Thanks," I answered, appalled at the conventionality of the exchange but with no other words. I walked limply back to the guest room and wilted into the bed. I remembered when I used to go into Leonard's closet when he was out of town, just to inhale his odor in his suits. The woody wool of Leonard's solid presence.

Polina emerged the next day, the day of the funeral, dressed in an elegant black suit, with a small hat and black veil pulled over her eyes. She was wearing a double helix of hearts Leonard once gave her for Valentine's Day. The two slender hearts outlined in gold were pierced by the same feathery gold arrow. At some level, I admired her sense of propriety, but I couldn't help thinking that Polina was playing the widow. She was playing Jackie Kennedy.

The ride to the cemetery was the most annoying. By then Tom had arrived, but Polina proclaimed that only the "two girls" would ride with her. So Joyce and I, dressed in dark blue, since neither of us had anything black, rode in the spacious limousine down Foxhall Road. Polina sat upright in her seat on the far right, so her back wouldn't hurt climbing in and out, with her eyes riveted on the road. Joyce sat in the left seat with tears streaming in thick globs down her face. In the middle, I looked around for tissue and was amused to discover two boxes of Kleenex, one pink and one blue. What a bizarre detail. What were the bereaved to make of the gesture? I did not feel bereaved. I felt, as usual, both conspicuous and detached.

When we returned home, Tom gave me a little card where he'd written: "This entitles you to a dinner and shopping trip in Leonard's honor." Finally, I cried.

———

At home, Tom took me to the most expensive restaurant he could find. I could tell that the gesture was thoughtful, but the restaurant was one my father would never have loved. The curtains on the windows were a bright red velvet. We ordered filet mignon, the most expensive item on the menu. Yes, my father had loved meat, but what was wrong? Neither Tom, nor I, had a drink. Neither I, nor Tom, had a joke. Neither of us spoke to the waitress except to say that we were here in honor of my father who had died. And of course the waitress didn't know what to say.

## *not out of concern*

Several months after Pat moved out of our Boston home, Tom's company was downsized. Since Tom was the newest recruit, he was suddenly out of work, on unemployment. I was relieved not to hear Pat's chirpy voice fluttering around Tom, but now the air grew brittle. He spent most of the day in his study. When I passed by his door, he was usually playing Tetris. "It's a computer game," he said. "You have to create a contiguous horizontal line as quickly as possible. Once you fill it out, it drops down. You are trying to stay low."

Games. I couldn't see the point of games. Why not let the screen fill up with blocks and see what design they made? I looked at the colorful array of tiny, moving blocks. Tom stared, unwaveringly, his hands clicking in a way that seemed frantic, disembodied. His intensity, his unsmiling face, frightening.

As always, I felt somehow implicated. Like when Polina's hair had been singed by the gas stove. That had been my fault. No one had acknowledged that a five-year-old would not know—not without having been told—that gas, collecting, would burst into flame on contact with a match. You had to light it right away, not wait. But I'd been so used to following directions without any sense of the whole that I was always accusable. I took responsibility.

Was it my fault that Tom had lost the job? No, I knew it wasn't. Perhaps my fault was that I didn't really take it seriously? But was that because I knew that, of course, he would get another job? Or because I'd never known anyone who had lost one? Pat probably did. Her father had been an alcoholic; she had a sister who was a drug addict. She herself had been married several times. But even in the movies, people who lost their jobs didn't sit in their studies in front of computers. I sensed that Tom was playing out a fantasy of being working class, and out of work. But the scene just didn't work. Our house was too big, our financial cushion too soft, the time he'd been unemployed too short.

Piles of paper teetered around Tom's desk. They seemed to be getting higher. He'd never organized since we'd moved from LA. Some of the piles had a layer of yellow dust on them. I thought that if I were going through the disorientation he must be feeling, I'd clean up the room. I'd do it for a sense of progress, of self-respect. Sometimes, I even suggested out loud that he might be pleased if he cleaned up his room. Grim lines creased away from Tom's lips and up his cheeks in cartoon arrows.

I didn't know how to react, trapped in an untenable crosshatch of response. For one thing, the arrows looked

comical. I would never have admitted that Tom looked like
a bad actor performing the role of anxiety. His performance
was all caricature. If he'd been in my play, I would have tried
to help him find a connection to his own life; I'd have tried to
make it come from inside, instead of this superficial drawing
of concern. I knew he would not be amused by my observa-
tions. Tom seemed lined in such acute angles that if I touched
any of them, he'd shatter into raging fragments.

I tried the gentlest approach I could muster (and it was,
I'd have to admit, gentle out of self-protection, not out of
concern).

"Tom, any luck?"

I hoped he could apply the question to Tetris or something if he didn't have anything else to report.

"Luck? Luck? Do you think it has to do with luck?"

"Well, no, I was just wondering how things were going.
Would you rather I didn't ask? You can tell me if and when
you want me to ask." This was a recent formulation I'd begun
to use. Just because I had a question or an observation,
I shouldn't assume that he felt like addressing it then and
there. It was a way of being thoughtful we had agreed, at
some point. I was so used to it now that I hardly noticed
that most conversation between us consisted of me asking if
I might talk to him.

One day Tom told me he had a "headhunter" working
on his case.

"Oh, good," I said but couldn't get out of my own head
the idea of someone actually returning from the hunt with a
string of skulls. I couldn't figure out who the trophy was.

"She got me a few options. But none of them pay nearly enough," Tom announced one night. I decided things must not be so desperate if he could reject possible jobs based on what he thought he should be paid. It seemed that he wasn't even going for interviews. It clearly wasn't my place to comment. Maybe, I thought, maybe he was just profoundly confident. He was certainly sure of his own worth. I was obviously wrong even to consider that he should at least interview. "Why?" Tom asked. It was not a real question, I knew. He returned to his study after dinner. A week later he told me that we had only one month of savings left to pay the mortgage.

Suddenly, I worried. I called Polina. I tried to make small talk first since Tom had insisted that we not tell parents. But finally I told.

"Tom's been out of work for a while. We seem to be down to the last bit of savings, and we're, uh, not sure how we'll pay the mortgage next month."

"Oh?" Polina said, distractedly. "I hope he gets a job."

Definitely not the response I had expected. I'd thought maybe I'd be criticized for something. For what? For not telling until now? For seeming to ask for help? I was stunned. Would my mother really not help? When I hung up, I cried. I missed the flowers Leonard and I loved in the backyard, missed the bunch of yellow roses he used to send for Valentine's Day.

But maybe, maybe, Polina's lack of response meant that the situation wasn't as dire as it seemed.

# equity

Then, Tom announced that he was going to take a vacation, alone.

"What?" My voice was louder and more horrified than I ever used. Shocked. I knew I must look odd, my mouth agape, eyes open too wide. It was so confusing. He'd never mentioned such a thing before. Had he? Had I, wrapped in my own world, missed it? And wouldn't travel cost money? How could he do that if we were in danger of not having money for the mortgage?

"I want to see Alaska," said Tom. "I always have, and why not start now when I have some time? At least I can do something I want to do." There was accusation in the last line. I felt a little as if I were being twirled around in a room of distorting mirrors. I couldn't tell how my perceptions could have been so inaccurate.

"I've made reservations," he said, definitively.

"Would you want to work in the travel industry as a job?" I asked, trying stay open, supportive. I knew that Tom thought I wasn't, and all I'd figured out so far was that I wasn't either as sympathetic as Pat might have been or as involved as his mother would have been. Tom's response took me off guard again.

"Get a job. You need to bring in money."

He'd never told me to get a well-paying job before. I suddenly realized that I must have missed some central point of Tom. High in starry clouds, buffeted by nursery-rhyme winds, I had floated, looking always for magic. Somewhere, I understood that I married Tom partly to be tethered. I counted on an unspoken agreement that he would hold my string and smile up at me from time to time.

In our large Newton house, I looked at the blank rooms, the soft white pines outside making delicate shadows on the deck, on the windows, the gracious staircase, the giant backyard, with its stern red oaks, the yard no one ever used. "Why do we need such a large house? Why can't we sell it, and live in a small apartment?"

"No," said Tom. "That's stupid. This house gives us much more space for much less money than any suitable apartment would cost. And we have equity."

## secrets, jobs

Then, secretly, as if that made it my own idea, I read want ads in the *Globe*. That very afternoon, downtown, I took a typing test and was sent out to a job at MIT. I met Margery, a professor, about a secretarial job.

"We would be lucky to have you as a secretary here," Margery assured me. Establishing camaraderie, Margery then mentioned her students' writing, their inability to follow one thought with the next.

"You know, Margery, I used to think that linear sequence, though I couldn't do it, was the mark of intelligence. Now I think that to capture the vicissitudes of the mind is more accurate and ultimately more communicative." Margery seemed intrigued. How smart I sounded to myself in light of Margery's interest.

At night, Tom and I lay separate on the new large bed, bought just before his layoff. It was designed perfectly so that one rolling did not disturb the other. There was no reciprocation at all, no dip in the middle. The bed kept us apart. I slept under a mountain of frothy quilt, and woke with a steamy head. Next to me, lying straight on his back, his face to the ceiling, Tom slept. His half of the bed was like a stately barge all night.

Wolf, lying on the floor on my side, was the first to wake, shortly before I did, with the acumen of a butler. He edged his husky self to the bed, as if his duty was to wake me, gently. Each morning, Wolf licked the fur between his toes, then lapped the milky white frock of his chest.

Dear Wolf. He'd come into my life like magic, after Pat and her dog moved out, before my father died. A man had come into the Waban Hardware Store with his large tawny retriever to ask Mr. Apelson if he'd put up a sign that the dog was for sale. The man was chatting with Mr. Apelson, and Wolf lay down on the wooden floor and looked in my direction. I found myself kneeling beside him, stroking his long calm side. How wise he looked, how devoted. He reminded me of Leonard from long ago, when I was a little girl and he was all that was silent and good. When I stood up, Wolf stood up, ready to follow me out of the store.

"He seems like your dog already," the man said.

"I know. He feels like mine," I'd said. I already had the sense of the two of us walking together down a country road, his long relaxed back near my hand, his face turning to me.

"I didn't even know I wanted a dog. I need to talk to my, to my husband. I'll take your number and let you know."

I knew I couldn't just take Wolf home, no matter how familiar and necessary he already seemed. I'd tried that once before. The month after Tom and I returned from Norway, when we still lived in Maryland, I'd bought him a puppy for his birthday. A small frisky black creature, with what was then, officially, my own money. I had bundled the pup up in a basket and presented him to Tom with a tiny purple collar on him. I was very proud of the sweet and unexpected gift. Tom had stared at me.

"Why did you do this?" he asked.

"What? I thought you'd love him."

"This is way too big a decision. We don't even know where we'll be moving." (It was before we moved to California.) "We need to make a decision like that together. What were you thinking? You can't just decide unilaterally," Tom said, almost patiently

It made sense, I guessed. It did make sense. I was embarrassed not to have thought of all that, only to have imagined Tom's smiling delight when he discovered the adorable wiggly thing. And instead, here was disapproval and head-shaking dismay. It made sense, I kept trying to tell myself. I wanted to be mature. But I couldn't stop crying.

So when I went to tell Tom about Wolf, I was sure he'd say no, almost counting on it, steeling myself, because I couldn't imagine myself turning Wolf down. Tom had sounded busy and tired.

"Look, you decide. I just want you to know up front that I will not walk the dog. I won't take it to the vet or do any of that stuff. I won't feed it either. But if all that is okay with you, do what you want." I hadn't expected to make the decision myself. Faced with it, I wondered how I'd deal with

Wolf's being sick, with his dying someday. But I knew that I had to have him.

Now, I could hear his nose sniffing at the top edge of the mattress every morning. Next he'd lift his paws to his ears, his collar jangling, his foot whipping at the ear where the thin membrane of ear pulled from the scalp. I would get out of bed, not disturbing Tom. Wolf would slide silkily to my side, his fur face against my leg. Then he'd plow his head under my hand and slant it down the mountain of his head to ride the scruff of his neck.

Tom's legs radiated damp heat, but he would not acknowledge me, pretending to sleep.

"You could make a salary. You should be able to bring in $30,000."

In a familiar mixture of defiance and acquiescence, I agreed that I could, to silence him.

Mitch, the administrator at the university, called the next day and offered me the job with a salary of $20,000.

"No thanks," I said almost too merrily, thinking I'd escaped.

———

Two weeks later, Margery called. She'd been out of the country. She wanted to know why I rejected the offer. The more I talked, the more Margery cooed and clucked and promised action. I was won over by her attention.

"If he calls with a better offer, I'll consider it seriously," I ended, pleased to be saying the words from the right script.

I hummed through the closets that afternoon, vacuuming doggy hairs, lining up shoes. I enjoyed the vision of Margery scurrying around the university on my behalf.

Even after I'd accepted the slightly better offer, I did not tell Tom. I waited over a whole night. I saw the moon shine on Tom's body and listened to Wolf's husky breathing.

———

At the end of eight months, Tom got not one but two job offers. He accepted both. He would soon be working all the time. He'd even negotiated a starting time of two months off and told me that he would be taking his trip before he started to work. It was a statement. Not open to negotiation.

# *mine*

At my new work desk, I stapled. Margery kept track of her own scattered thinking by demanding the return of pink slips on which she had written individual instructions with some kind of mark to indicate that I had completed the tasks outlined on them. The pink papers were insistent, against the cobalt blue of my blotter. Also, there was a pile of documents to be Xeroxed in the photocopy room. There were notes saying what I must do today, and in each case it was urgent and should have priority. My officemate, Angela, began to chat at me. I angled my head stiffly toward the computer screen, hoping my posture spelled out: *Person at work trying to decipher difficult codes with too little instruction in too short a time. Beware.* But Angela, a big-breasted middle-aged woman in 1950s secretarial garb, little heels, and thin calves with no discernible muscle, was a caricature of her job.

"Oh, these kids are just so nervous the first week, don't worry, they'll settle down." She meant the professors, I realized.

Angela continued: "I just picked up a rib roast, on sale, for my husband. My son signed up for a series of good courses, I hope he does well." On and on, she trotted past invisible social signs I'd posted. After all, I knew how to respect other people's signs of impatient dismissal. I'd never have trespassed on someone huffing and puffing as I was. It was unnerving to have someone in close proximity not notice. It was even more unnerving to be the one needing someone else to adjust.

"Angela!" I said finally, as directly as I could, "I can't think about what you are saying." I was embarrassed at my own words. "Please, I'm sorry; there's just too much."

Angela fell silent. Though a little chagrined, I was also a little pleased.

I was besieged with instructions. The other secretaries counseled: "Cheat on the lunch hour, they take enough out of you."

"Play dumb," Wendy said, "the less they know you know, the less they ask. Keep smiling, they're little spoiled children. Handle them as you would children, just that, children, spoiled but with tenure."

"They give you as much as you will take, so be sure to stop when you need to," Mary Jean summarized.

Mary Jean, it turned out, had acted in plays, had been married, divorced, strung out on drugs in California, and recovered. She was working full-time and going to school full-time. Mary Jean seemed to have some credibility.

When I managed to get one correspondence typed and printed on the computer that was still only a week old to me, Margery scanned it rapidly with her gray eyes.

"That! That space!" she said, her voice high and tight with betrayal. "That space is too small. Put another space there!" she said. I returned to my desk, humiliated, dedicated in some awful and familiar way to pleasing Margery.

One morning, before any professors had arrived, I tried to organize my day, taking each paper off the pile one at a time, to see the scale of work. One sheet of paper lay still in my hands:

```
Room for rent. I want someone to live in my
one room studio for six months. Completely
convenient, Beacon Hill, small garden apt,
with small garden. Bedroom, living room and
kitchen, fully furnished with just enough
furniture.
                                        Lisel
```

Lisel was a professor who would arrive in the middle of a sentence into my office and complete it, laughing. She weaved the names of children's books into her economics treatises. She wore a black slicker and giggled, she'd made puppets and been sought after by foreign dignitaries. I liked everything about her. I sat still, staring at this paper not even addressed to me. I folded it, folded it again, smoothed the creases, as I'd seen Tom do, when he sent letters. It was interesting to be so proprietary. I creased the neat square into smaller and smaller sections of paper and felt the walls disintegrate around me. My married walls dissolved into small brick walls, my size.

What if I could have my own room? A single set of cutlery, with a tiny fork, like the set Leonard gave me when I worked in New York. What if my groceries could be single-sized? One small wrapped slab of fish. Only my own two legs crossed. My one curly head, on one fresh pillowcase, one deep sleep at night. My two hands, smoothed with nighttime hand lotion. My one heart beating steadily through orderly and impulsive days.

What if I let go of the money and the Newton township Tom and I lived in, with its own private lake in the summer, its green raked lawns, its motored snow blowers cleaning sidewalks, its mailings reminding its women to have breast exams, and, in tidy green plastic boxes, its dutiful collection and recycling of bottles?

What if I left my familiar but inaccessible Tom? Left the possibility of him running neck and neck with me over rutted roads on some vacation? Left his breath warm at my back, always there, always able to overtake me? What if I left the campfire bacon we might sizzle—if we camped, if we ate bacon? What if I were no longer to perpetuate my hand, for instance, repeatedly sliding up and down the polished mahogany handrail in our colonial house but instead dwelled entirely inside my own self, taking my own self barefooted upon sand or high-heeled up the steps of some hotel? What if I were to depend upon my own self as that which held me instead of Tom's tall and conventional appearance? What if I were to live in this apartment for rent?

The second week, some of the "girls" invited me out to lunch. In a bubble of hair, we moved slowly, our coats brushing, as if we were one organism.

"Chinese, right?" said Rita.

"Right, hon," said Wendy.

"So, how is it so far? How are your bosses?" Wendy bulged up against my arm.

"Fine," I said, monosyllabically, unwilling to give anything away. Their hips were wide over the narrow wooden restaurant chairs. All five of us ordered chicken lo mein. I ate lots. Even this seemed a new permission. Rita twirled the cabbage to the edge of her dish. Angela hadn't been invited. Angela had mentioned that "those girls" had their main meal at noon, since they had no husbands, no one to go home to. Not like her and me.

Rita, munching happily, launched into a mini-lecture.

"Have you got a parking spot? Get one. You can get anything right now. Go for it. It won't be so easy later."

"But . . . but . . ." I sputtered. Years of Tom telling me to take public transportation cracked like spring ice.

"Go ahead. Tell Mitch you need it, you're golden just now." Mary Jean smiled. Her eyelashes were individually tinted, her eyes pale blue; her voice tiptoed across the table.

"My father's an Irish fisherman at Revere Beach," she told me one day. I found her daringly self-made.

After three weeks, I began to scoot my orange office chair, confidently, from side to side over the rug cover. I treated myself to an ice cream after lunch, ambling across Massachusetts Avenue, back to the office, passing students and other secretaries. With one arm full of papers for Margery held in a single gigantic clip, the other holding the cone way out in front, to drip on the pavement, I encountered

Mary Jean coming the other way. "Oh ho ho!" said Mary Jean, ostensibly about the ice cream cone. It felt as if I'd been swooped up in multicolored feathers. Maybe I could make it on my own. Maybe things would work out, and there would even be celebrations.

# PART THREE

# 1984

## love him?

Huge flakes of snow, the first of the season, floated outside the window in no hurry to land when I walked into the restaurant where Mickey was waiting. Mickey looked a little like a country western singer, with dark curls, very tight blue jeans, and boots. He wore a ruby earring in one ear. It fit with his dark pirate beard. His handsome long-sleeved shirt was clean and finely woven. His shoulders were surprisingly muscular for a teacher, and his legs also were lean and fit, though short. I first met him months earlier, when he came to see a girl in one of Margery's seminars do her presentation. I was standing with the girl, Jody, when Mickey walked up to praise her. She'd been his student in high school. Jody asked about Annie, Mickey's partner. I was standing there when Mickey told Jody that Annie was very, very sick. Margery introduced me as an assistant who helped with her writing.

Mickey said he'd love to talk to me sometime about how I went about editing writing. I wasn't sure I had much to say on the subject but agreed to meet him for coffee sometime.

Now here I was at our meeting. The place was near our house but a different world from the glossy mahogany-furnished restaurants Tom and I usually patronized. I'd entered some new terrain of people who were invisible on the upscale Newton streets or in the high-priced malls with their high ceilings. Who were all these people hunched over meatloaf dinners at 3 p.m. on a Saturday afternoon? Some of the women were in hairnets, focused intently on their plates. When I saw Mickey, smiling from the corner, his sapphire eyes shining, I felt both safe and daring.

We ordered one rice pudding to share. We'd be dipping our spoons into the same little dish. The distracted waitress, who set it on the table, with tea for each, was clearly not going to bother us. We were as private as if alone. I took in the full calm presence of Mickey, who looked as if the afternoon was altogether open, with no distraction.

Almost without preamble, Mickey asked if I loved my husband. Ordinarily, I'd have been offended by such a direct question. Ordinarily, I wouldn't even have considered its content in my haste to avoid the direct inquiry. But Mickey looked patient and interested, not selfishly inquisitive, not wanting to summarize. He sat across from me, one hand open at his cup, the other arm draped over the shoulder of his chair. The angles of his body expansive and welcoming, his arm embracing the chair. Snow drifted steadily out the window. There was a quiet pause in the conversation, and

neither of us made a move to leave. I understood that at
some level, I was determining whether it was safe to proceed.

I realized I had never even asked myself if I loved Tom.
It had gone without saying. Hadn't it?

Tom had returned from his Alaska trip uneventfully.
He hadn't called the three whole weeks he was away. He'd
explained that he just wanted some time not to have to report
in. "Do you love him?" Mickey repeated, presciently, I felt.

———

I didn't answer directly at first but told him how I'd been constricted as a girl by the stockings I wore in high school, the
garters that stretched down my thighs so that at every step
they stretched, they also retracted. Was I unaware that I was
describing a marionette? I told Mickey that across the street
from my house then, there was a stucco house with a thin
old man and a frail blond woman. Once, I knocked on their
door and was invited in. The woman had asked if I'd like to
see the ballroom. I remembered entering the vast slightly
moldy room with earth-colored tiles shaped like fleurs-de-lis
and grand columns. At the far end was a large veiny mirror
and on one wall a magnificent gold screen with a floral motif.
The old woman presented the ballroom with a sweet grin
and a grand gesture as if this secret ballroom had been saved
for me. Also, there were porcelain dolls seated around the
room in long satin gowns. The old woman had picked one
up, one with brown hair and a sapphire dress. The woman
had held the doll, with its long dress swooped down from

her arm, gently, her head nodding slightly, her other arm, with its fluttering cuffs, gesturing faintly toward the room. This one is like you, she'd said. I told Mickey this and, in his relaxed listening, I went on in a long arc toward answering his direct question. Why had I never told Tom any of this? Why had I never been allowed the leisure of circumlocution? Until now, no one had ever asked.

Across the street from the magic house, I went on, I had ridden silently every Saturday with my mother and sister in a car filled with Polina's cigarette smoke and purpose, to shop for dark tailored clothes for school. And my shoes, I even mentioned those brown Oxfords that made a square-heeled chunk of embarrassing sound when I walked in the library or at school. I knew that Mickey would understand about the embarrassment. He taught chemistry at a posh school in town, he'd know about the agonies of adolescence. He nodded with a little smile as if he certainly did understand how small sensitivities could loom for a young girl. And his eyes glistened sympathy.

Then I found myself telling Mickey what I had never told anyone before, about trying to leave Tom when we still lived in California. I'd gotten a cheap flight to see a friend in Cleveland and then just kept going, all the way to Cape Cod. It was years ago. I didn't exactly remember how it had happened. I was pretty sure I'd convinced myself that I just wanted to take advantage of the cheap flights and see the Cape again. But once there, the relief of being free of something was palpable. It was as if I had taken off like a large bird and landed on the very edge of the East Coast, having tried my own strength, ready to risk cold or turbulence. I told Mickey that from Cape Cod, I had called Tom to announce that I was going to try to live on my own. I had determined that I would get a place, find a job, as a waitress maybe. I dimly remembered that the words were coming to me as I spoke them out loud, gaining credibility by being voiced. If I could so quickly, so flexibly, come up with a possible scenario, maybe I could come up with a life. Tom, on the other hand, as if he were steadying hysteria, as if he were the experienced captain of a cruise ship used to the way the women turn at the tropical moon and prepared to rescue them for their own salvation, had said in a low and unadorned voice, "You get back here right now. "

Mickey's silence allowed the gravity of the moment to register. I, hearing myself, suddenly reconsidered. Did I really attempt escape? And having tried, why did I let it fade so quickly? Why did I never mention it, even to myself? It must have been that Tom was so calm, so certain; so, I now realized, so menacing. In Mickey's presence, I began at last to register the outrage: that Tom had never asked me why I wanted to leave.

I remembered that Tom's response had seemed right at the time. What did I know about life, his lack of interest implied. Did I really expect that I could become a waitress, with no experience at all with such work? It was all fantasy, wasn't it? I was not a wanderer, I would not know my way. I needed Tom standing in the doorway, large, rectangular, his head a dark shape, didn't I? Afraid of my own ineptness, I had returned to California, to life with Tom. Neither of us had ever asked why I'd left.

Now it was only serenity, the snow falling, the tale unwinding, loosening through my hands. Mickey seemed to have all the time in the world, no rush, no preoccupation, only kindness and some mysterious understanding of me, of women.

## motion pictures

The next week, I invited Mickey to MIT under the guise of showing him around. I showed him the small, carpeted seminar room next to our office and led him to the corner of the room not visible from the door, though most of the administrative staff had left for the day and the students hadn't started to roam the halls, as they did in the evenings. Mickey and I swooped together in a movieland embrace. His arms held me with so much strength I could have arched back in happy ecstasy as we sank all the way to the floor. I noticed the stiff short bristles of the rug on my stockinged legs, my whole body sensate, alert. Mickey kissed me, lingering on the very edge of my lips. He brought me to a sense of the huge open well of my mouth, and I felt deeply grounded and bounding toward him, both, at once.

Just before our lips touched again, Mickey said, "I wonder about Annie and this."

Mickey murmured between kisses that Annie lived with him in his house, but "we sleep in separate rooms. I stay with her because she is sick and I've promised." He smiled a relaxed lusty smile. I was again propelled toward him with no thought but the resounding space he offered.

Later, Mickey explained more about Annie.

"She's very very sick. She'll either get a replacement kidney and be fine or not, and die." I couldn't tell quite how he felt about these alternatives.

"Either way," Mickey continued, looking down, a curl curling down his forehead, "my father abandoned my mother for another family. I won't do that to Annie."

He spoke with such tender patience and fortitude that I decided it was all worked out and need not really concern me. It was between them. I'd had enough of sanctimonious commentary about how people should behave.

Now I saw how alien the *via negativa* life with Tom had been. When he'd proposed with "I can't think of any reason not to marry you," I had laughed, thinking that as a mathematician and logical thinker, Tom had systematically eliminated obstacles to his premises. It was his way, and I had translated it to truth. But now it felt impoverished.

———

Back at our house after my snowy afternoon with Mickey, in the middle of the night when the snow stopped, I ventured out for the pure joy of it. I allowed myself the pleasure of taking a walk without having to present a case to Tom in support of my whim. Even that was thrilling. I walked through fresh powder, from glow to glow of streetlamp light. I stopped at a single frozen drop that was gleaming like amber. The stars were icy in the midnight sky. Standing under the dark dome of sky, I felt myself sharpen into crystal. The years of dull anger and vague gesture clarified. I would leave Tom; I would own myself.

The plan unfolded. In the morning, I would talk to Mary Jean at work; she probably knew the name of a lawyer. I would move myself out of the house in Newton rather than disrupt anything for Tom. I didn't want him to have any cause for complaint. I'd take Wolf, since Tom never liked him. I would escape with Wolf, into the open; we would go on scent.

A few days later, when I met Mickey, I told him my plan. He was not surprised. "What part of town would you like to live in?" he asked.

———

What part would I like? Had I ever asked myself this simple question? This was so practical, so different from the years of laborious hesitation, rationalization, and counter-argument I was used to, that it reconfirmed my decision. Wearing his red scarf, Mickey was a merry hearth. An unexpected warmth filled me, as Mickey moved with me to the next step, so different from Tom's sluggish reluctances.

That Saturday, Beacon Hill was covered with bright cold snow. Mickey and I, supplied with a list of apartments for rent, had a brisk lunch of chili and beer in a pub on Charles Street. The winter sun splashed on the dark wooden tables. I watched

Mickey's cheeks warm to a deep hearty smile. Late that afternoon, after a number of dark, small studio apartments, we
walked into an apartment on Revere Street with thirteen windows, the sunset sun pouring in one pink bank of them. The
front bay windows afforded a meager view of the Charles. We
looked at each other and instantly agreed that I would take it.
I felt as if I was in an acting class improv, some delightful com-
edy ending, in which all the timing brought laughter. I would
be able to walk over the Charles in the morning to MIT.

One act led to the next. I was not aware that I'd thought
any of these things through, and yet I was behaving as if I'd
laid elaborate plans over time and now, finally, some obsta-
cle removed, was carrying them out. I'd be able to move into
the new apartment in two weeks. Now I was close enough to
escape, and sure enough of a destination, that I could tell Tom.

I wrote him a letter announcing that I was leaving. The
letter went through a number of drafts, getting smaller, more
direct, each time. I didn't want to give him any premise with
which to disagree and render my conclusion invalid. I found
myself crossing out lines, whole paragraphs of explanation,
and just announcing that I was leaving. At the end, there was
almost nothing for him to question.

Dear Tom,
    I need to leave our marriage. I think that we are not
doing each other much good. We seem to be existing without
animation. I hope that by leaving, I will free us to discover
the next segment of our lives, and to live more fully.

I knew the letter was strange. There was so much I couldn't say. I couldn't say "it was clear" that we were doing each other harm, even though that was the kind of language he would use, the kind of objective-sounding all-encompassing claim of reality, since he would surely disagree with my statement. So I'd settled for the more tentative "I think." To Tom, the fact that he walked right by me when he came home from his jobs and straight up to his office, where he spent the time until dinner playing solitary computer games, was only evidence of how much he still hated his work, not evidence that we had nothing to say to one another. My weak suggestion, once, that perhaps he should change jobs, was met with fury. He'd insisted then that he couldn't find jobs that paid as much as his did. But why did we need so much, I wondered, looking at the large empty house, gazing at the enormous backyard that he entered only once a year to help with the leaf raking. He would not back down from the accomplishment of the large Newton house, the clear evidence of success.

For me, though, it had been three years since I'd spoken without asking permission to interrupt, during which I had felt myself an interruption in his life. I hoped Tom would at least sign on to the notion that there was not much animation. I hoped that the word *free* would resonate with him, he seemed so constricted. I did wish for liberty for us both. I was sad that the letter was so terse, so unexpressive; but that was the point, wasn't it, that I couldn't express myself to him. Any life in my letter would be pounced on.

"I can hardly breathe. Your dour mood is draped every-where in this house, and over me. I feel like I'm in plastic, protected from everything and running out of air."

He would want proof of my ridiculous melodrama. How could I prove it to him? And when I couldn't, he would have me, defeated. I couldn't see any way out but this wan little letter.

I gave him the letter the next afternoon. I meant for us to sit together to read it, but he read the letter while he stood in the upstairs hall, between the door to the bedroom and the door to the bathroom. The day was cold, the room gray; Tom's jaw was tight, his thin lips thin. He read quickly, then said, "I will not fight with you."

As usual, I tried to fill in the blanks. He must have meant that he would remain dignified and right, that I was wrong. I was wrong because he was such a good husband. He had told me this, frequently. Wrong, mostly, because I had struck preemptively, without even declaring war.

# *snow*

Now I scurried around the apartment on Beacon Hill to make my nest. The wind was blowing the Charles River into gusty white waves. It was snowing again. It snowed and snowed, so even the river was covered with white. The sky moved close, blanketing the old Beacon Hill streets. I waited, soft as snow, for Mickey to come to his first dinner in the apartment. The city had dropped away, and the old radiators whistled and hissed heat into the room like wind. My years of blunt hands seemed to soften, and I noticed, with new attention, the wood square frame of the chair, the very ridge of the log it came from.

When Mickey arrived, the air burned with cinnamon candles and with clarity. In my tiny kitchen, whatever cabinet door we opened produced the next ingredient—a jar of roasted pepper tomato sauce, a half package of thin spaghetti, an onion. With hardly room for two in the kitchen, we passed close but not touching. The energy between us swirled the pasta plump in the suddenly boiling water. I did not remember ever cooking with Tom.

Then on the sofa I'd taken from Newton that would serve also as my bed, high over whitened Boston, with the window blinds wide open to the river and to anyone who would see us, we drank from dark blue goblets of wine. Our words spilled over in the night. We spoke at once and back and forth, laughing about books we'd read, about my choices of what I'd brought out of the house in Newton, about the deep night sky. Grinning, we sought each other's eyes. I was about to leap into the unknown chasm of Mickey. I was standing on the brink, and nothing held me back.

On the dark sofa, with the starlight staring through the window, we threw our clothes off our bodies like used shells, peeled ourselves to glowing skin. Mickey's shoulders were white above a seaweed sea. His mouth rode the rim of mine. Best, best was each unfolding, each refolding. Our legs sought our legs. I rode with fingers, with tongue, the histories of Mickey's chest, the hard curved scroll of his muscle. Mickey drew me into his delicious mouth. His fingers raced, rapid as deer scampering, over the mossy cleft of me, soft padding, strumming. Best was each inhalation, each exhalation. Best was every silence. Best was Mickey's face close at my belly. A spray of brilliant plumage erupted in me.

Then we lay as if in a meadow. Mickey leaned on his elbow, his head on his hand, and an ocean rolled beneath. Poseidon-like, his beard was wet with whitecaps, his rock-blue eyes accounted for the domain.

# balancing (the checkbooks)

J ames Kirkland, the divorce lawyer Mary Jean suggested, was, to my relief, taller even than Tom. His office was full of bronze statues of waterfowl and painted birds, some decorator's idea of a hunting motif that inspired confidence. I understood that James had enough substance not to cower from Tom, not be intimidated by his certainty or by his ability to formulate and express his designs. I told James right off about the attempt to leave years ago, the attempt I had conveniently forgotten until I'd found myself talking about it to Mickey.

"You are doing yourself a service in leaving this marriage," James assured me after he'd heard my story. One of the first steps would be a financial disclosure from Tom. I was amused. There would be nothing to disclose, I told James, jauntily.

Predictably, Tom was prompt—gleeful, almost—in response to this particular request. All his checks were already stored in numerical order, his payments were categorized by type, by date, by percentage of the not-too-fluctuating whole. I almost bragged to James that Tom would not conform to his experience of male conniving.

"To a fault, almost, Tom is upright, honest," I claimed. "He balanced our checkbooks to the penny every month." The only "discovery" to be made would be my own engagement with the financial realities of life.

For the first time, I imagined taking charge, remembering figures, making my own little charts, in pencil probably. Preoccupied thus, I was dumbfounded when Tom's figures announced that suddenly, he was making 25 percent less a year than he had been.

"What happened to him?" I asked James, not suspicious, frightened. When I read, with James, that Tom was earning less, my first sensation was fear. It never occurred to me that the decline might be voluntary, not with Tom so adamant in never again wanting to be out of control, with a fat savings account growing ever more plump.

"Right on schedule," James said with a wink, explaining that a lowered salary meant a smaller alimony payment, unless James could prove that some deal had been struck, like lower salary, higher bonuses, or some other way of disguising a deal.

When Mary Jean learned that I had left the house I'd shared with Tom, she warned me to take all my old journals. It was the first time I considered Tom's possible interest in them. He would never read something private. Would he?

"What a bastard," said Mickey after I told him the story of the letter I'd found from Pat. And after I explained Tom's refusal to move to a smaller place, to redesign our lives based on what we actually loved instead of what looked impressive, Mickey was direct.

"Nonsense. Of course it costs less to live in an apartment, especially if you own and rent out part of your house and have no mortgage to pay." Mickey, a landlord himself, whose figures lurched across a page, sloppy pencil slurs, tracks diverging, showed a route utterly different from Tom's calculations, displayed in regular columns, finished, professional, and wrong. Mickey's way was working, clearly.

My old explanations of Tom drifted underfoot like shriveled shadows. At night, I dreamed about empty houses. Was Tom always absent? There must have been times of abundance, maybe in California. But when I tried to remember, I remembered only that Tom was not with me when I cycled to the shore. Now, when I tried to remember the kitchen there, I remembered only that there were roses on the wall along California Street. I remembered walks toward the Palisades, streets planted in all the same species of deciduous, or dark blocks of pines with buoyant arms of dark needles, choreographed and anticipated by giant Santa Monica trucks that swooped in to sweep the fallen pine limbs after a storm. Was he there at the supermarket? Or at the farmers' market where the waffles were? We did go together to an Armenian restaurant. There was an aquarium with a large white fish floating indolently and the smell of stale meat. Did we talk?

How could I have forgotten every conversation?

———

As the date of what would have been our fifteenth anniversary approached, I remembered our sixth anniversary. "We have a successful marriage," Tom had announced, making an uncharacteristic speech. "We have a lovely big house, two cars, our health." He'd elaborated on the size and prestige of the house. I had drifted, contemplating a new awareness of him as the child of failed farmers. I wondered if he was joking when he spoke proudly about our two cars. He didn't mention me. My hands had remained on the linen tablecloth in the restaurant. I stared at the glass of crystal ice and realized that he was serious.

When I called Polina to announce the separation, I was nervous. "I don't know how to tell you this, Mommy, but I have decided to leave Tom. "

"Oh?" said Polina "Well that's fine. We never did like him very much."

It was anticlimactic how uneventful the telling was. "I hope you've got a good lawyer. Tom might be difficult."

I said goodbye and held the phone in my hands, astonished that my mother could be so accommodating and still offer no camaraderie.

————

Now, Tom was tall in his suit, on the other side of the courtroom for the first step of the divorce procedure. He did not look at me but walked back and forth on the other side of the corridor, wearing a sky-blue jacket, a relic from the sixties. His expression was grim. At one point, he came alarmingly close. "You know you will regret this," he whispered. I heard his brittle hurt.

———

When late that night Mickey called, ripe as cherries squeezed, we put funny names on Tom, names that contained him, names that he did not easily leak out of: Tomsmug, Tomslug, TomLeastSaidSoonest. I laughed in my Beacon Hill apartment with a gusto I'd not ever heard. Mickey was teaching me to mock.

# *synchronicity*

When spring came to Revere Street, the whole street burst into linden flower. The Junior League girls and their rambunctious swains began to swarm the old lamplit streets. All night, their spring-drunk voices coursed through my open grated windows.

Then, suddenly, my month-to-month rental was sold as a condominium. I would have to move. I was ready; the charm of Beacon Hill, now that I could see and hear the people around me, had paled. The window boxes I had discovered when the snow melted, bulging with miniature daffodils and slender red-and-white-striped tulips interspersed with trailing arborvitaes, now showed limp yellowed leaves and candy wrappers.

Mickey had begun to look for a new place for me when, right on cue, the apartment next door to his and Annie's suddenly, inexplicably, became vacant. Everything was so easy, so mutually convenient. I would move next door to Mickey, next door to Annie, in Cambridge. My revived faith in the synchronicity of events made this seem reasonable.

I did not realize until I actually met Annie that I had not really believed in her existence. Annie seemed an offstage character. But she was large as life. She walked with a cocked inquisitive head, her whole body skewed slightly in a pose of perpetual curiosity. In her straight gray hair and pastel Dutch clothes with lollipops and lambs, she seemed like a pleasant kindergarten teacher—that is, until the subject of children came up.

"We don't have children, Mickey and I," Annie announced early on, "because kids are spoiled brats who eat you alive."

I was startled by her self-confidence, her flouting of conventional sympathy, especially since Mickey was a teacher. But this attitude of Annie's helped. It meant that I could be the one who loved life. It meant that Annie might reject lots of the usual expectations. It meant that maybe it was going to be just fine to be next door, in some Bohemian ménage à trois.

Annie actually showed me around their apartment, so I saw with my own eyes the separate bedrooms. Annie's was a sweet colonial hideaway with tiny, flecked wallpaper, an old-fashioned bed, and a nightstand piled high with cellophane-covered library mysteries. Mickey's was a small back room with a boy-sized cot at an angle in the middle. All around his bed were shirts and underwear and toppling piles of folded clean clothes. The contents of Mickey's room seemed to have been thrown in, like pick-up sticks. His room spoke of a lack of permanence; it was open to possibility, to change. Annie's, in its heavy order, was stodgy with certainty.

What most surprised me was Mickey in Annie's presence. He was diminished. Physically, he shrank. Annie seemed to take all the space. She was only a little taller than Mickey, but she stood like a queen in her kitchen, which was in the center of the house. She prepared meals. She purchased Mickey's clothes, his nice shirts, and hemmed his jeans so they didn't drag. She called him to dinner and gave him a plate with the portions all served. I learned that when Annie left town, she prepared all of Mickey's meals, labeled them, and put them in the freezer. Annie was tolerant of but not impressed by Mickey's teaching; tolerant of him, as if he were a small frisky pet. Mickey walked with his head drawn into his shoulders. I decided that Mickey's remaining with Annie must be about fealty—in feudal terms, what the knight must do, no matter where his personal affections tended. He was serving an ideal; this explained the look of subservience. And further, it allowed me so much scope. I would be loved, treasured, but would have air around me, and mystery. My house would be always clean and fresh when Mickey came. My bed made, white and floral, a bower for him. This situation, unusual though it was, with our proximity, with my willingness to wait and to appear to be off to the side, suited me perfectly.

I imagined myself Solveig in *Peer Gynt*, waiting patiently. Yes, I would see him through the drama of Annie's illness, of her eventual death, and then we, having done the right thing, would move to the next phase of our lives together. So I settled into the apartment next door. I wedged my bed under the eaves of the window that faced Mickey and Annie's house. At night I rose up, like a flared cobra, and saw directly into their bathroom window, which was covered only by a white half-curtain. Fortunately, I never saw her, only Mickey, and only the top half of him. I wondered why he did not look up. He must have known I was there, my face white in the window.

From my second-story porch, during the day, I could look directly into Annie's garden, the peach and apricot trees, the towers of raspberries, the several species of failing and healthy blueberries, the chain-link fence full of goose-berry, and six varieties of tomato, including pear-shaped yellow ones. Annie was a collector, a domestic scientist. She conducted rigorous research on anything that rose to the level of her interest. Mickey's comment about this intimidating tendency was that indeed Annie must control everything in her domain. I, battling envy of Annie's competent attack on the world, wondered then if it was my spontaneity, my ability to shift with the shifting nuance instead of following a rigid line of investigation, that attracted Mickey. He loved my willingness to move in next door, to yield to circumstances creatively. Mickey told me often that Annie had no interest in sex. Sex was boring to Annie.

The rules of encounter emerged with a kind of inevitability. Because I got the liquid pleasure of my time with Mickey, I drew a veil over myself in Annie's presence. Annie could not only be right about her choice of the best popcorn and the finest ice cream, she could be the best shopper, the most proficient and energetic cook, even the most intelligent of us. Mickey and I deflected any questions Annie might

234 REBECCA KAISER GIBSON

consider about us with a mutual effort, by reflecting Annie
back to herself, in glory, from any angle.

I didn't pause to consider how familiar my role of self-
effacement was. It felt different. It was a game I was playing on
purpose and with Mickey. It was a conscious choice. It was
acting weaker since in fact I had all the real power; Annie
didn't.

In the early afternoons, by daily arrangement, Mickey
and I met at the local gym. We left our houses at separate
times and met, as if by accident. When I entered the work-
out room, I felt Mickey even before I saw him. Stretching
one muscled arm across his chest, he glanced over his bulky
shoulder, keeping recognition out of his face. As I sauntered
over to him to the beat of the music in my headphones, he
looked quickly, appraising. Then, sotto voce, made some
comment.

"Do you see that guy there? He can't keep his eyes off
you."

When I'd look at the guy in question, I could not actually confirm what Mickey said. But maybe he was right. He
claimed to have insight into the male psyche. It was kind of
thrilling. I was astonished at my delight at parading around
the gym in my leotard, with my private music playing in the
Walkman, keeping me focused on something internal while
I was being observed. I mounted my favorite equipment, the
one I hung down from, aware that when I descended, my
waist would be pulled to a long thin willow of itself. I did
so, languorously. No one criticized what seemed to me like
rampant exhibitionism. On the contrary, it was normal and

sexual in the gym. How far I had come from the stilted life at my parents' home, from my embarrassed entrance to adulthood, from my dry marriage. Sex was not at all boring to Mickey and me.

# *how could it be wrong?*

On the way home, we walked and chatted together until we reached the corner. This tension and release was ecstasy, I thought. Shifting like clouds, like weather. We talked about everything without having to ask permission, about the view of the sun on buildings, about Annie the night before, and what was actually going on for each of us, about the school where Mickey taught. Mickey's perspective on the divorce proceedings, and on Tom. Mickey was always protective. He anticipated Tom's defensive strategies; he pointed out the discrepancies between what Tom claimed and what he did. He quoted Whitman. He was in favor of multiplicity, abundance. At the corner of our block, we decided who would go ahead and who would linger, in case Annie or anyone else was there to witness our return.

Sometimes, Mickey called with an invitation to go out to dinner with him and Annie. When Annie was in the room, his voice seemed to have a rod down the center of it. I did not cut lilting scallops of melody into my voice, as I did when he called in the morning to tell me that Annie had left and that he would be right over with his breakfast. Mickey did not romp around in his sentences, as he did when he arrived at my door with enough fresh raspberries for the two of us to have over pancakes or with the bowl that he filled with a few berries, some milk, and some dregs of cereal to leave on his own counter at home as evidence that he had his usual breakfast and not the one with me.

We agreed to go to an Indian restaurant in Harvard Square. I was surprised to have Annie order for us. We had just established that we would share, as is usual in Indian restaurants, when Annie announced that we would begin with vegetable samosas. It was as if Mickey and I were children. Hansel and Gretel, our hands touching under the table, our expressions wide-eyed as the world appeared before us.

Noticing a decorative shelf in the corner of the restaurant lined with a row of large jars, golden globs bobbing in them, I'd blurted, "Aren't those lovely?"

Unimpressed, Annie explained, "They're brandied peaches. I make them for New Year's."

It wasn't long before I was in Annie and Mickey's living room almost every night, sprawled with their dogs and Wolf on the floor, watching *Jeopardy!* I listened to Annie answer the questions. Sometimes I wondered if I was lying when I didn't confess that I hated the cheese quesadillas Annie served with such panache, the fatty white cheese foaming out of their corners. I hardly ever addressed, even to myself, the ultimate lie of sleeping with Mickey and eating with

Annie. I had not talked to anyone about this threesome, this new life of mine. When I did try to celebrate my relationship with Mickey, in one of my infrequent conversations with my sister, Joyce was horrified. She sided promptly and without question with the wronged woman. She pointed out that I was living a lie—the lie was that no one was telling the truth. Joyce couldn't see, wouldn't allow for, my new animated life full of surprises with Mickey. Or the domestic comforts in Annie and Mickey's living room or the pleasure I got from the power of knowing so much more than I let on. The final magic was that I shared my knowledge with my lover, who was there also. I felt lean, beautiful, and full of complexity.

Often, after *Jeopardy!*, Annie sat at her desk in the room that was meant to be a dining room but now had a craft desk for each of us. At Annie's desk, the colored pencils were arranged in rainbows. She'd filled a notebook with illustrations for fairy tales. She was working on Snow White and Rose Red. The two little girls had on dirndls with tiny blunt flowers. Every so often, Annie showed Mickey and me a page. At Mickey's desk were stacked boxes and boxes of beads, sorted and stored. He had been making beaded necklaces that he sold at craft fairs. I loved his entrepreneurial spirit. There was something one could do that was fun to make money. It was all so different from the stultifying predictability and gloom of Tom's work. Mickey invited me to make a necklace, and Annie nodded. I had the feeling that Annie liked the three of us to spend time in the dining room at our quiet tasks. I had a little table near Mickey's. I made a necklace of beads of blue cloisonné interspersed with bronze balls, to go with a pair of earrings. It was the first time I'd really looked at earrings, at how they were put together. Even my curiosity was waking up in this benign permissive world.

Mickey took me with him to a gem and jewelry show. He told the woman at the desk that I was his assistant. And now I was brushing by women in so much amber that their bodies leaned backwards to support the yellow weight. Before my experience with Mickey, I had dismissed the ugly plastic appearance of amber, thought it tawdry. Now I understood the worth and rarity of the dangling strands of oval ambers that descended from both sides to the central one, the "queen." The women, dressed in white velvet pants and polka-dotted jerseys, with gaudy emerald rings; the men in tropical Hawaiian shorts that flopped limply on skinny legs. Their turquoise belt buckles, greenish turquoise string ties, and outsized turquoise rings unnerved me. I didn't know how not to condemn them as tasteless. I didn't really know which standards to use: the ones from Tom, which seemed needlessly critical, or the ones from Mickey, which seemed to have no edges.

My hands swept across a table of pearls, pinkish ones meant for tawny skin and straight silk hair, nacreous mother-of-pearl, lustrous as camellias, icy white, cool to the touch, white after white. My fingers over the twined shanks fed my eyes. My eyes leapt in waves, in the whole seascape of pearls. I felt I was swimming in garnets, peridot, periwinkle, tourmaline, heliodor, pools of color. I was sinking into what felt, for the first time in my life, like happiness.

# 1986

# telos

Alone in the evenings, I began to take notes following the dictionary derivations of words. I had come upon the word *telos* by accident, overheard it somewhere. *Telos: End. Purpose. Ultimate object or aim.* Writing the definition, I thought perhaps it was time to consider the ultimate object, or at least the aim, of my relationship with Mickey. *Telescope*, I continued, reading down the definitions, *far seeing, afar off, at a distance, to look.* Again, it seemed uncannily accurate. It was time to add more distance, more vision to my outlook. But then I read the next definition, of the verb, to telescope. *Telescope (v.) To force or drive one into another.*

## oh!

Then, Mickey told me he was going to move out of his house.

"Oh!" I gasped. It came out like the sound of someone being punched. So I followed it with another "Oh" that sounded more like a casual encouragement for him to keep speaking. Mickey, who was usually very sensitive to nuance, joking with me when I didn't sound enthusiastic enough about him or when I didn't sound bitter enough about Tom, didn't seem to notice either "Oh." I was frantically whirring through options, though only seconds had passed.

Mickey, who could take a single word and stroke it and flip it and flatten it and growl it so the word became a premise for and the shape of a whole session of lovemaking, Mickey told me, simply and ominously, that he had a lot to work out. "Actually," he said, he would "just move into the apartment on the first floor of his house." The tenant had been told to vacate in a month. Mickey said he didn't know how it would end.

"End?"

There had never been talk of ends, only of days. No, only of hours, hours that seemed to last forever, with only the boundary of Annie's comings and goings.

"I've got to be free," Mickey told me, "to follow the leads."

"OK," I said, making rapid revisions, rapid editing. I had just been thinking about the whole shape of our relationship. Maybe this solemnity, this preoccupation on his part, was appropriate. Maybe, maybe he was really thinking deeply about moving our relationship onto a more formal, more public plane. I was not sure I even wanted the public part. I was not sure why he would need to follow leads. I'd have thought I was the first and main person he'd want thinking with him. But maybe Mickey wanted to know that he came to all his conclusions himself, without my influence.

But wait, wouldn't it be much more awkward for me to appear to be visiting the two of them if only Mickey was downstairs? I'd obviously be seeing him. Surely Annie would suspect something. Still, Mickey probably wanted to know that he'd be near Annie if she needed him, if she got sick. I could imagine such a scenario, but it didn't really ring true. I felt so responsive to Mickey, not interested in opposing him. Obviously my role must be to give him space. That's what Annie didn't do. Annie crowded him. Annie kept the TV on, watched shows Mickey had no interest in. Annie brought library books for him to read. Annie decided where they went, what they talked about, what they ate, what they thought. And at the same time, Annie's kidneys were acting up. She was visiting the doctor more often than before. Her body was swelling with the mounting poison. She was trying medications. She was dominating and helpless at once. No wonder Mickey was morose, I concluded. I didn't want him to think I was in any way like Annie. I would get out of his way, try to clear and light the path. I was dimly aware that I'd reverted to some role. I was vaguely aware that I was scared.

Now, though, I could see from Mickey's eyes, which stared forward, which looked like Tom's eyes, that the conversation was over.

———

That night, Mickey invited me over with a lilt, again, in his voice. I could see from my window that Annie's car was gone. I wondered if everything was magically back to normal. Mickey was sitting at the far end of the living room, soldering gems onto bits of rusty nails to make the new line of jewelry he'd started.

Together we'd bought boxes of rusty tools and fasteners in junk shops, and he'd treated the rusted bits with fixative all winter, so they wouldn't rust on people's clothes. Now he was putting garnets in unexpected locations and stringing nails on silk threads. This line hadn't sold well immediately, but I prided myself on my ability to know, as soon as they walked into Mickey's blue art-show tent, which women would be interested in the unusual pieces. Often they bought the necklaces I had modeled.

I settled into the couch opposite Mickey, remembering those times with tentative pleasure, and picked up a few books. This was usually Annie's place; I knew I'd broken an unwritten rule in sitting there. Mickey's face was deeply concentrated on the work, so I began to look at his magazines on shamanism.

"Silence," Mickey remarked, "there is usually so little here, at this house. I always want to unplug the TV."

"Yes." I didn't know how to go on. His words might be an endorsement of me, of the quiet space I gave him, but his voice sounded so edgy that I couldn't really relax. I hoped he was thinking that in his own place, maybe our place, he would have it as he liked.

"I like to throw things up in the air and see how they land," Mickey said, breaking the silence that had settled again.

"Yes," I echoed. I loved this spirit of his. Suddenly, I wondered if this strange conversation was a preamble to a marriage proposal. The brooch he'd been working on was now cool enough to touch. It was a tiny pair of forceps, with a small blue stone in the eye of the joined tongs.

"What I want is a real family," Mickey announced, suddenly.

At first my heart leapt. But Mickey was detached, preoccupied; he was not really addressing me. Maybe he meant his own mother and brother, that he wanted more contact with them. This constant translation I needed to do was unsettling, to say the least. Mickey continued.

"I want someone who does not leave at graduation. Someone who will care forever." My first reaction was panic. Did Mickey want a child? Was I ready to give up my precious time alone with Mickey, once we finally had it? I was surprised at my reaction. But he did start by speaking of throwing things up in the air. Maybe this was just more of the wonderful way he complicated things. We both heard Annie's steps on the stairs at the same time. I slipped down to the floor, continued to page through the magazines, and left soon after.

I spent the next day, a Saturday, wandering around Cambridge, noticing children—with more attention than I had for ages. It took some effort to see them as real; they were all so well-dressed, they looked like plump hothouse tomatoes in multicolored caps. Such well-cared-for, handsome little toys of the well-to-do. But by the end of the day, I'd begun to imagine life with Mickey and our child. I'd put us all in the scene: Mickey racing down the street, swerving a baby carriage with hilarity and joy. A cottage somewhere, a child crouched outside examining a salamander. Mickey loved salamanders and would really get into them with a child. All of us at night, with Mickey rolling on the floor and playing tag with the child in the rough-and-tumble way he did with Annie's dogs and with Wolf. I was aproned in this scene, smiling in a silent sweet-smelling kitchen and loved by both of them. At night, with the baby asleep, he would make love to me. We would talk and talk about the day. By the end of my walk, I was transformed, ready to tell Mickey, "Why not?! What a great idea." I was proud of my flexibility, able to go from rejection to delight in such short order.

———

Our next meeting was accidental. I saw Mickey at the gym in the morning. He never went in the morning, so I hadn't expected to meet him then. He was neither excited nor dismayed to see me, and this discouraged me from launching into my news. Mickey joined me at an adjacent exercise machine and began to talk. "I just need to stop acting on my desire for approval and affection from women in power."

What was he talking about? Every time I saw him, now, he erupted out loud in what seemed the middle of a different conversation. What women in power? Did he mean Annie? How was he acting on a desire for her approval? If he was indeed planning to move out, how was that acting on a desire for approval? It seemed the opposite. Who would approve of his moodiness? Anyway, he certainly didn't mean me. He had all my affection and approval; he didn't need to earn it.

On the way home, at the corner, Mickey brought up the topic from the evening before. "Yes, maybe two children."

"How would we do that?" I blurted, feeling my new tolerance preempted. He'd actually already determined the number—without even talking to me?

"Oh," said Mickey, turning to me as if noticing me suddenly, "but not with you."

I almost shouted, "You are planning how many children you will have, but not with me?!"

Mickey shrugged. I realized that I might not have picked the most important thing to say, but I was too disoriented to know what that might be. I felt ripped open, and that the pain was just coming to the surface. Mickey was like a dragon with a long lacerating tail slicing my body, and here was the worst—that the wounds were almost unintentional as he turned away, so focused on going wherever he was going.

# *telos*

The next day Mickey came to my apartment. He was stretched out for his after-meal nap on the couch under a crocheted blanket that Polina made. Because he said nothing, I finished the dishes and, trying to reenter the conversation, asked him if he'd had any more thoughts about family.

"Yes. I had a dinner with Jane the week before last. Remember Jane?" he asked. "And her two children?"

"Jane?" I said. "Jane? Dinner? Jane?"

I had no coherent thoughts, just the sense of falling fast down a well but not landing, just a rapid and terrifying descent and no clear thought to stop me. Suddenly, I was speaking.

"I don't think you just had a dinner with Jane. I think, I think—"

I was dimly aware of repeating myself but more amazed at the puzzle I had just, then and there, put together.

"I think you've had a number of dinners, which is why you're never here anymore."

"Well yes, we've had more than one dinner," Mickey conceded.

"I think, I bet," I found myself almost yelling, "you are sleeping with her!"

Mickey said nothing.

"I think that's why you've stopped sleeping with me. That's why you want two children; there already are two children."

I was discovering these thoughts as I said them. How could he decide in the abstract that he wanted children and then take on two who happen to come along with a woman who couldn't possibly matter to him? It was all so calculated. I couldn't yet bear to think about what this all meant to me.

"That's right," Mickey said, calmly.

"And what do the children think about that?" I shouted, trying to confront him with his own illogic. Mickey responded as if some mildly interested third party was querying him.

"Well, the younger one really seems to love me. She's like me, adventurous. Loves to climb rocks, wants me to teach her guitar. The older one must still miss her father. She is very rude to me and disrespectful to Jane."

"How old is she?" I interrupted, seething.

"Thirteen."

"Well, what do you expect?" I noticed that I was almost hissing, sound was bubbling against my teeth.

"I guess you'll want these back," Mickey said. Reaching into his pocket, he handed me the extra keys to the apartment. But he owned the apartment. I took the keys.

"Shouldn't we hug each other?" I asked, knowing that it must not be right to be initiating this forced embrace but not knowing how else to think.

When Mickey left, I stood in the middle of the living room, unable to cry. The floor had dropped out from under everything. Where was the surface of reality? How could I breathe this air that had gone? How much stability I had assumed with Mickey; how little there was.

# *ready*

Then Wolf became suddenly, unaccountably tired. He still looked up at me when we walked outside and stepped when I stepped, but when I stopped, his hindquarters sank to the ground as if he were exhausted, even early in the morning. Something had happened to him. On Saturday night he needed to go out and couldn't get himself back up the stairs. When I called the vet, I was told to carry Wolf up the stairs and back into the apartment in a large towel. "He's an old dog," the vet said. "Follow his lead."

Wolf's loyal, skinny legs dangled out the front of the towel sling. His nose was still cool to the touch. I watched him, sprawled in the living room, breathing heavily, though he hadn't moved for hours. Pity for him and self-pity trickled down my face when he moaned a low sad sound and stretched his fine snout on the floor. Wolf, who had been my loyal protector and comforter, who had accompanied me everywhere with gallant attention, needed me to help him.

I whispered into his fur ear for him to give a sign of what he wanted. "If you are ready to die, dear Wolf, let me know and I will do whatever you need." I wondered if I had to say the words out loud. Soon afterward, Wolf asked, by gesturing toward the door, to go out. So, I carried him in a large white towel down to the little yard. He stretched, silver in the moonlit night grass, quietly. When I turned to go back up, he did not glance at me as usual, but far off. Several times in the night, I woke up and ran down the back steps to check on him. But he had not moved, not all night. Every time I came down, he was looking calmly beyond the fence, beyond the trees. I stroked his soft sides but did not call to him. I felt I should not distract him with any demand.

In the morning, I brought him a bowl of water—it had been two days since he'd drunk. His snout moved toward me, toward the bowl, and he took one lap of water before he slid his neck back onto the slightly cooler grass under it. He had not moved except to drink the single swallow of water. I knew it was time.

When Wolf died, he went from patient labored breathing to peace, in an instant. I felt him leave his beloved body, a pelt then, quiet on the ground, while the real Wolf was swept up and into my heart. Wolf was the guardian of my horizon, galloping at the tide's edge with salt wind in his grand tail.

The next day, I called Annie to tell her about Wolf's death. We hadn't spoken for weeks, not since Mickey had moved downstairs, and of course, we had never really spoken. Annie seemed truly sorry.

"He was a good beast," she said, "loyal and true."

I heard all the clichés, but they were right. In contrast, Mickey had begun to seem like a circus sideshow. Annie confided that Mickey was out of town.

"I think he is having an affair," she said, laughing, as though it were a joke, so inconsequential an act as to be mocked. "He's off at the Cape, probably with her."

"Yes," I corroborated, "he is."

"You know," Annie continued, as though nothing particularly momentous had been said, "people thought you and he were lovers."

I was looking out the window, up at the bright clear sky. Suddenly, the path seemed simple. "We were. It's over now," I told her.

"I thought so." Then she said, "I am sorry about Wolf."

When I hung up, I felt a new strange calm, as if the ground were flat, and I standing, simply.

# speaking up

All the weeks that I had been occupied with Mickey's inconsistent behavior, I had fielded calls from my mother and sister. Polina, in her perpetual self-reference, reporting on various problems she had. A room needed painting. She'd got the gutters cleaned, but it "cost a fortune." Her little left toe had an ingrown nail. She had to go to the doctor. She'd coughed up some blood. She didn't know how to find new tennis partners now that Leonard was gone. All topics of her concern were presented with equally urgent intensity. Who could she get to screw in a light bulb in the overhead hall light?

"Who have you tried?" I sometimes asked, but Polina just changed the subject. She was taking a Senior Education class, on Shakespeare, what did I think of that?

"She's senile," said Joyce, on the phone. "She's had another car accident. She mustn't be allowed to drive!"

"Wait a minute, wait a minute." I could hardly attend to the situation without Joyce's outraged imperative about "what mustn't happen, what must be done" coloring it. "Wait, Joyce, tell me about the accident first."

Joyce told me that Polina hit a curb in a parking lot trying to back out. "She doesn't even look behind her when she backs out of the driveway! A child could be there, walking to school. She could kill someone! We've got to stop her. If we go together, we can get her doctor to forbid her driving."

"Joyce!" I finally interrupted. I felt, again, as if I were about to take the wrong strand from the argument; still, at least I'd got hold of something. "No children even walk down that street to school. It's way too dangerous to come from Cherry Lane."

After I spoke, I realized that it was true. Also, that the scenario of impending and horrific disaster, while possible, was not always inevitable. I realized that I knew something about possible disaster. And I knew something about other outcomes. Even this thing with Annie and Mickey had turned out so differently. What was amazing was how it felt to tell Annie, suddenly, as if the sky cleared. I'd been looking out the window while talking to Annie, and I saw the sky, blue, simple, straightforward. I, who had always thought I'd only thrive, possibly, in mysterious regions, was relieved to just be standing in the room, with the blue, with the truth told. It felt like being free of Tom's heavy invisible grip.

Joyce was unconvinced; she thought it unethical not to stop the disaster she imagined.

The discussion was cut short by what happened next. The blood our mother had been spitting was traced to lung cancer. Polina took to her bed, sleeping through whole days when she didn't have doctors' appointments. Elsie, who had remained with Polina for twenty years, started calling each of us sisters on a regular basis to report in on the patient. The car stayed safe and idle in the garage.

Joyce took on the detailed management of the household. When she visited, she left lists in the kitchen of what medicine Polina was to be given, and when. Joyce hired the night nurse and interacted with the social worker assigned to Polina. Joyce decided that Polina was depressed, that's why she wouldn't get out of bed. She needed psychotropic drugs. Joyce was becoming a social worker herself. Once the drugs were prescribed, Joyce told Polina she'd have to cut out her evening martini.

———

Polina's martini would be the last ritual to go. She'd finally stopped smoking, after all the years of her adult life. The house had a quiet cool smell instead of the acrid weight of old smoke that I'd grown up with. Polina stopped knitting her wild loose sweaters in front of the TV. The TV itself, the most current model, outsized and triumphant, always booming at top volume, always presenting Polina with mechanical challenges—"How do I get it to change channels with the hand-held shifter?"—was off. The house was silent.

Polina lay all day in her huge bed, getting smaller and smaller. Still, at around six, at the hour when she and Leonard would convene on the porch in the summer, in the grand living room in the winter, she sat up in bed and waited for her martini. Each night's nurse had been taught, more or less, how to make the martini. But now, with the drugs, Polina was forbidden to have her drink.

One night I got a call that Polina had fallen out of bed and refused to be returned to it. She seemed dazed, drunk. The next day I called, intending to ask Polina what had happened, see if she wanted more able night care, consult with her. I found myself adamant that Polina not be presumed upon, not be second-guessed.

So rarely consulted about my own desires, here I was, protecting, in this fierce and unasked-for way, my mother. But when Polina answered the phone in her new, tired voice, when I heard recognition dawn in Polina that it was me, and she said, "Hello dear"—this was new, recent, this "dear"—I realized what I must do.

"Mommy"—this was still what we called our mother— "I think I know what's happening. I bet you are sneaking downstairs to make your martini. You don't have to sneak, Mommy. We can stop the depression drugs and you can have your drink."

"Thank you, dear. That would be better," Polina said, relieved.

————

I was amazed. Such a turnaround! Such a lot of turnarounds. That my mother would be sneaky. That she would admit it. That I was giving her permission. And she was accepting it so graciously, without argument! That I had guessed right and released her from lying. It all seemed part of an unintentional campaign to clean out the cobwebs of my life: Annie and Mickey, and now Polina. Not to mention that I, who had resented my mother's sloppy drinking all my young life, was now inviting her to drink. What difference did it make if Polina had a drink, even if she got drunk, if she had a moment of pleasure on the way?

When I hung up, I also recognized that it was the second time in a short while that I'd confronted someone about a subterfuge that I hadn't realized I saw through until I acted. It was new to have no secrets, no secret distance from Tom, no secret connection to Mickey, no secret speculations.

# ah ha

Joyce and I sat in parallel chairs at Polina's bedside. It had been years since we'd both been home at the same time. It was the first time we'd ever sat beside our mother's bed together. Polina was no longer wearing her glasses; her eyes were a clear hazel olive color. She was no longer wearing her hearing aids, so the room was relatively silent, no high-pitched out-of-tune squeal. It was cocktail hour, though there were no drinks, only the sun beginning to set in the bedroom window. A week after I'd given her permission to have her martini, Polina stopped noticing cocktail hour.

Polina's hair had turned, since the radiation and in the absence of beauty parlor visits, to a soft cottony white web over her head. It had been shorn, and much of it that had fallen out now grew back in a soft mat. Elsie usually put a bandana on Polina's head, at a rakish angle, but it had fallen off and Polina seemed oblivious.

Polina had a small sweet smile on her lips. She was wearing a coffee-colored satin nightgown that Elsie had dressed her in. Her legs were so thin now they were barely visible under the covers. Polina looked from one daughter to the other, deeply and sweetly. She looked winsomely and with great concentration at me, then at Joyce. I wondered if this was a profound moment, if Polina was about to give us a message. She started to speak.

"I understand," Polina said, importantly, and smiled again, victoriously, "one of you has glasses, and one doesn't."

The statement was so startling, so anticlimactic, so revealing that we both laughed, like water, like a brook. The setting sun sent a sliver of light across the foot of the bed. Polina settled back, pleased.

She slept through that day, and through the night. Joyce took the room on the same floor as Polina's room; I was on the third floor, out of hearing range, and able, actually, to sleep. At dawn, I was awakened by a gentle hand on my shoulder.

"Our mother is dead," said Joyce.

Walking downstairs to Polina's bedroom, I felt that the house had already changed after Leonard's death. And now, as with Wolf's death, a weight had been lifted. What was left was this tidy woman, lying on her side, chastely, in her clean and pretty coffee-colored nightgown in a neatly made bed. Polina hadn't moved since the morning before when she drifted into sleep. Her face was calm. The smile was gone but so was the anguish.

Later that morning I found myself opening the shades in the room. I didn't stop at the exact halfway point, where Polina had always insisted they stay, but let them flutter up, up to the very top, so the light, for the first time in decades, fell in over the dark floors and then, in the fresh breeze from the open window, sailed over the top of the bed. Light crept even into the closets, a cheery little strip over her sandals, reclaiming the seaside scent of *rosa rugosas*, of sand, and of my own life, pulsing.

# acknowledgments

This book has been nurtured by readers over decades.
Without the unwavering belief in the project of Lilla Gilbrecht Weinberger, I might well have abandoned this book years ago. Kim Cooper, Michael Downing, Joe Hurka, Mark Karlins, and Mary Sullivan each added helpful responses to early versions. Jim Gutensohn and Joanne Kauffman listened to chapters with admirable patience. Later, Jude Sales added her delight. I am grateful for my dear friend Loudon Seth and for Diane Klann for sustained and sustaining enthusiasm. And to Catherine Pilfrey for friendship and support. Thank you each and all.

Thanks also to Bill Clegg, whose thoughtful rejection of an earlier version of the manuscript kept it alive.

The literate and insightful attention of Jill Betz Bloom enabled me to carve out the narrator, to see her dimensionally, and to embrace her limitations. Alexandra Teague's acuity has been a treasure always – a buoyant breath of confident wisdom.

My accomplished cousins have supported me, it feels, unconditionally: Bob Kaiser, Hannah Jopling, David Kaiser, Patti Cassidy, Charles Kaiser, and Joe Stouter. Sarah Hyams, and Tema Silk each have attended to and responded to my writing with precise and precious attention. Paul Kaiser my mirror cousin and I discover each other over and over again with astonished relief. That Sister Ellen Keane hears my heart has certainly given me the energy to come home to this book.

The seemingly fortuitous assistance of Scott Edelstein lifted the book out of obscurity and guided it to a smooth landing. For introducing us, as well as for her all-around profound presence in my life, I thank my amazing and thoughtful sister, Tamara Kaiser.

From the start of her life, Zoe Randol has uplifted me. From the start of our marriage, Charlie Gibson has encouraged and believed in my work—including the addition of "Grand Silence," the guarantee of uninterrupted work time in our shared life.

Finally, especially and essentially, Linda Lindgren has shepherded this book into its physical reality—joined me in guiding it and celebrated its being.

I am indebted to the team at Arcade Publishing—working with them feels like a miraculous co-creation. In particular, I deeply appreciate the dedicated, careful attention of Cal Barksdale, editorial director.